BENDY®

JOEY DREW STUDIOS®

EMPLOYEE HANDBOOK

UPDATED EDITION

BY CALA SPINNER
AND PAUL DAVIES

SCHOLASTIC INC.

Joey,

After much thought I have decided that it's time for me to move on from the studio. Let's discuss as soon as you have an opening on your schedule.

I hope you'll understand, old friend.

—Henry

To: Henry Stein
Joey Drew Studios

Top five places I'd like to go to when I (finally) get out of town:
1. California
2. Athens
3. Rome
4. Giza
5. Anywhere but here—

Groceries to pick up:
- Bacon
- Red potatoes
- Onion
- Butter
- Ground black pepper
- Salt
- Dried parsley
- Milk

To-do list:
1. Finish preliminary sketches
2. Leave note for Joey
3. Clear out files
4. Have a nice, hot bath at home

DREAMS COME TRUE

Welcome to

JOEY DREW STUDIOS®

Dreams

It all starts with a **DREAM.** The dream is the spark which sets the wheels in motion. You just have to believe that anything is possible. That's how all cartoons at Joey Drew Studios start.

Come

When we all **COME** together and work hard and happy, the impossible gets created. This is the part where everyone gets to play their role in turning dreams into realities we can all enjoy.

True

When our masterpiece is finished, we behold the new **TRUTH** we created. Our dreams are now a reality, and ready to share with everyone who wants to be happy.

Joey Drew

WORK
HARD
WORK
HAPPY

Photos © Shutterstock: splatters throughout: (Anastacia-azzzya), (DigitalShards), (ESB Professional), (EVZ), (GriyoLabs), (iadams), (WitchEra), papers throughout: (Anelina), (Feng Yu), (Gosteva), (hidesy), (I. Pilon), (Karramba Production), (LiliGraphie), (nunosilvaphotography), (Picsfive), (Rudy Bagozzi), (showcake), (Valentin Agapov), 1 background texture and throughout (Lukasz Szwaj), 2 paperclip and throughout (AVS-Images), 2 envelope (Mark Carrel), 2 coffee spills and throughout (Juhku), 3 top right drips and throughout (Kirill. Veretennikov), 5 banner and throughout (bodabis), 5 texture and throughout (Milos Djapovic), 9 torn paper and throughout (s_oleg), 13 photo frame and throughout (Popartic), 13 tape and throughout (Odua Images), 14 texture and throughout (Bruno Ismael Silva Alves), 59 warranty paper (Artist_R), 59 receipt and throughout (Jill Battaglia), 73 cup ring (schankz), 97 papers (Mark Carrel), 143 splatters (xpixel).

ISBN 978-1-339-03226-9

10 9 8 7 6 5 4 3 2 1   24 25 26 27 28

Printed in China 38

First printing 2024

Book design by Amazing15

Featuring Artwork by Firion Bifrost, Prismahays, AtAt, WhicheverComa, Katie Guinn, Shannon Marie, NoisyPaperDragon, Nao Sasaki, MissPeya, Merkurfisch, Cary, Weretoons, TimetheHobo

Additional illustrations by Abby Bulmer

CONTENTS

Part I: Surviving Your First Week

Part II: Welcome to the Studio!

Part III: Bendy and the Dark Revival

Frame (00218)

Frame (00298)

Frame (00308)

Frame (00315)

Frame (00374)

Frame (00415)

Frame (00423)

Frame (00462)

Frame (00484)

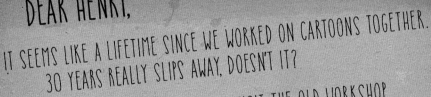

DEAR HENRY,

IT SEEMS LIKE A LIFETIME SINCE WE WORKED ON CARTOONS TOGETHER.
30 YEARS REALLY SLIPS AWAY, DOESN'T IT?

IF YOU'RE BACK IN TOWN, COME VISIT THE OLD WORKSHOP.
THERE'S SOMETHING I NEED TO SHOW YOU.

YOUR BEST PAL, *Joey Drew*

SURVIVING YOUR FIRST WEEK

Congratulations on your recent employment with Joey Drew Studios! Now that you're officially part of the team, you'll want to know everything there is to know about working here. And why wouldn't you? It's the best place in the world to work!

In this section you'll discover some of the studio's state-of-the-art tools and facilities, as well as the cartoons you will be working on. In the weeks to come, hold fast to this helpful manual—it can be a real lifesaver!

We do what we can to cover all our bases in this employee manual, but as protocols and personnel change, feel free to add your own notes and updates to this guide. As you meet new people and learn new things, it can help to ask questions of your coworkers to make sure you have procedures down pat. A studio is only as strong as its weakest link, as Mister Drew likes to say, and an inquisitive mind leads to a better tomorrow!

CHAPTER ONE
"MOVING PICTURES"

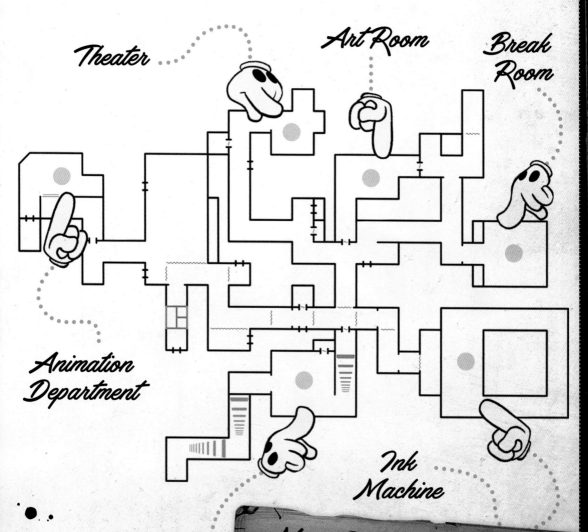

Theater

Art Room

Break Room

Animation Department

Ink Machine

Lunch Room

New Objective:
DISCOVER JOEY'S SECRET

From: Joey Drew

Memo to Staff Regarding the Ink Machine

People often ask me what sets Joey Drew Studios apart from your average Joe Schmoe Studios. Why, it's our wonderful staff, of course, but how can we take our work to the next level? I present to you ... the Ink Machine!

The Ink Machine is the latest in artistic technology, custom created in conjunction with the Gent Corporation just for us. This marvel of a machine churns out high-grade, fine-quality ink and pumps it throughout the studio like a steady, beating heart. This ink can be used not just for drawing, but also for creating usable, life-sized productions of, well, just about anything you can think of!

Why might we need our own Ink Machine, you ask? Excellent question! A gourmet chef doesn't use second-rate ingredients; no, she carefully selects the finest goose liver for her foie gras to avoid committing a faux pas. Actually I think foie gras is disgusting, so let's rephrase. Macaroni and cheese. Now what's better: Macaroni and cheese made with whatever cheese you can scrounge up at the corner deli, OR macaroni and cheese made from a blend of finely aged Gouda and Havarti?

Think of the Ink Machine as the vessel for your gourmet cheese blend. This ink can be placed into the newly installed "Ink Maker" machines around our studio, to print whatever you'd like—a wrench, a radio, a gear, a plunger, you name it! Because this ink is the crème de la crop in the ink world, it can also enable you to render illustrations so crisp, so real, you might think they could actually come to life. Can you imagine?

Directions:

Search the decaying workshop. Along the way you may locate several items of interest.

- **Bacon Soup:** When your health is low, eating a can of Bacon Soup will instantly restore it.
- **Audio Logs:** These recordings were left by employees of the studio for you to listen to.
- **Radio:** Each chapter contains a radio you can turn on and listen to. You might even recognize some of the songs!
- **Punch Card Stand:** Punching in saves your progress.

Follow the overhead signs until you come to the Ink Machine Room. You will need to collect and insert two dry cells to power the lift. The batteries are located to your left, one inside the trunk and another on the shelf. Insert them into the power module to the right of the lever, then pull the lever to activate the lift.

BEWARE THE INK MACHINE

New Objective:

FIX THE INK MACHINE

Now that you've activated the Ink Machine, you will need to repair it and turn it on. To repair it, head to the Power Station Room, where you'll learn you need to gather the following six items:

1. **GEAR:** Return to the Ink Machine Room and open the chest to the left of the doorway.

2. **BENDY DOLL:** Sitting on a chair in the Theater.

3. **BOOK:** Head downstairs to the Lunch Room to find *The Illusion of Living* on a table.

4. **INK JAR:** Back toward the entrance, find the ink jar on a desk beneath a "Work Hard, Work Happy" poster in the Animation Department. You can also spot a fun Easter egg at this desk—the animation cel on the desk changes each time you wander away from it.

5. **RECORD:** A light will turn off in the room containing the radio. Once it does, you'll be able to enter and retrieve the record from underneath the desk.

6. **WRENCH:** Inside the open chest of the life-sized Boris the Wolf.

To: Staff

Happy Holidays from Joey Drew Studios!

Another year at Joey Drew Studios has certainly brought us closer together! No one could have foreseen the many triumphs and challenges we've come upon this year, but one thing is for certain: We'll weather any hardship, and celebrate any victory, together.

In the spirit of the season, I'm asking each and every one of you to donate something from your work station—an object that means something to you and stands for who you are, the essence of what makes you, you. I've laid out some pedestals in the break room for you to leave them on. With any luck, we'll be able to appease the gods to bless us with another successful year.

Wishing you and yours a joyous holiday season to reflect on all you're thankful for.

Voice of
WALLY FRANKS

At this point, I don't get what Joey's plan is for this company. The animations sure aren't being finished on time anymore. And I certainly don't see why we need this machine. It's noisy, it's messy. And who needs that much ink anyway?

Also, get this, Joey had each one of us donate something from our work station. We put them on these little pedestals in the break room. To help appease the gods, Joey says. Keep things going.

I think he's lost his mind, but, hey, he writes the checks.

But I tell you what, if one more of these pipes burst, I'm outta here.

TOP SECRET

Interacting with the
Ink Machine

We're proud to have such advanced technology as the Ink Machine available in our studio, but be advised that this machine is both expensive and sensitive. Please refrain from interacting with the Ink Machine unless you have received express permission from our resident Gent repairman, Thomas Connor, or Mister Drew himself.

In the unlikely event of a burst pipe, ink pressure can be turned down or off completely using the pressure valve in the rear of the Theater. Subordinate valves throughout the studio can also help drain ink from a burst pipe, but should only be used in emergency situations. Please alert

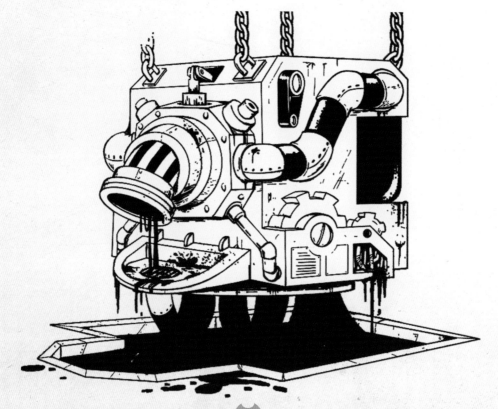

our janitor, Wally Franks, to any ink spills, and tell staff to avoid the area until Mr. Franks can clean the mess.

Should you require ink, consult the weekly Ink Output Schedule that's posted for your convenience. Ink is piped directly to your work area, so you should not need to visit the Ink Machine itself for any reason outside an emergency.

Voice of
THOMAS CONNOR

It's dark and it's cold and it's stuck in behind every single wall now. In some places, I swear this godforsaken ink is clear up to my knees! Who ever thought that these crummy pipes could hold up under this kind of strain either knows something about pressure I don't, or he's some kind of idiot.

But the real worst part about all this . . . are them noises the system makes. Like a dying dog on its last legs. Make no mistake, this place . . . this . . . machine . . . heck, this whole darn thing . . . it just isn't natural.

You can bet, I won't be doing any more repair jobs for Mister Joey Drew.

New Objective:
TURN ON THE INK MACHINE

After placing all the objects on their respective pedestals, head to the Theater and turn the ink pressure valve. Then return to the Power Station and flip the switch.

OVERACHIEVER!

A few achievements will be given to you through the natural course of the story:

PICKING UP THE PIECES: Collect all the pedestal items.

HELLO BENDY: Fall through the floor.

But before you head to the Ink Machine Room to finish *Chapter 1: "Moving Pictures,"* be sure to check the following items off your to-do list:

CROONER TUNER: Turn on the radio in the room where you found the record.

THE CREATOR: To the right of the life-sized Boris the Wolf, walk straight through the wall containing the "Sheep Songs" poster to find a secret room and theMeatly.

THE PAST SPEAKS: Listen to all the audio logs in this chapter. There are two: one from Wally Franks in the narrow room next to the closet, and one from Thomas Connor after you fall through the floor (after returning to the Ink Machine Room).

THE TASTE OF HOME: Collect all the Bacon Soup in this chapter (see page 15).

STUDIO LAYOUT

BASEMENT

ELICIOUS!

BRIAR LABEL
BACON
SOUP

Made from a traditional family recipe Briar Label Bacon Soup
tastes just like the home kitchen cooking that mom used to make

"JUST THE WAY THE LITTLE DEVIL LIKES IT"

12 CENTS

THE TASTE OF HOME

There are twenty-one cans of Bacon Soup scattered
throughout the studio in Chapter 1. Be sure to get
them all for "The Taste of Home" achievement.

- One can, lower drawer of the dresser.
- One can, under the projector.
- Five cans, downstairs closet.
- One can, on a shelf to the left of a door.
- Four cans, in the closet beside Wally Franks's
  audio log.
- One can, inside the closet full of projectors.
- Three cans, on the shelves beyond the projector.
- One can, under the projector.
- Two cans, on the shelves to the right of the desk.

After falling through the floor . . .

- One can, bottom of the shelves containing Thomas
  Connor's audio log.
- One can, left of the transmutation circle in the
  Ritual Room. (Tip: Avoid the transmutation circle
  when walking into this room, or else you will trigger
  a cutscene.)

Bendy!

Allow us to introduce you to the mischievous little devil who started it all: Bendy! By now, we're certain you've noticed that Bendy is the face of Joey Drew Studios. A playful little fellow, Bendy can get up to some naughty antics when left to his own devices. Luckily he has friends like Boris the Wolf to keep him in check.

Bendy is our star, the biggest cartoon character currently in production. Throughout the studio, you might find movie posters or cardboard cutouts of Bendy recycled from various theatrical promotions. Beware when opening closets—some of our more playful employees have rigged Bendy to jump out at you!

Bendy also features in various inspirational posters or workplace reminders. We love our main squeeze, and we think his constant, vigilant watch is a great reminder of the care we put into all the characters at the studio.

Directions:

After turning the pressure valve and flipping the switch on the Power Station, be sure that you've finished everything you need on this level, then visit the Ink Machine Room to turn on the machine. You'll notice some inky footprints leading from the Ink Machine Room into a locked door at the end of the hallway. You will find the Ink Machine Room boarded up, at which point Bendy "will present" himself.

New Objective:
ESCAPE THE WORKSHOP

Survive long enough to make your way back to the entrance, and you will fall through the floor.

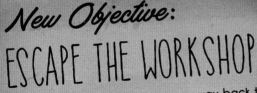

New Objective:
DRAIN THE INK

Wade to the valve located in the corner of the room and turn it to drain the ink. Head through the doorway and down the stairs to locate the second valve. Continue downstairs to find the third valve. Once the ink drains, you'll be able to enter through the doorway and locate the axe.

Safety Precautions

Joey Drew Studios is proud to say we have never had a (bad) accident on the job. But due to insurance requirements, we are obligated to stock our studio with the tools you need in the event of a natural disaster, fire, or flood that might require evacuation.

AXE

In various points of location throughout the studio, axes are available to help if you ever need to clear a path to an exit. While some offices have frivolous things like fire extinguishers and first-aid kits, we are proud to offer our employees the best of the best . . . an axe.

IMAGINATION

We pride ourselves on hiring staff of incredible ingenuity. Should an intruder enter the building and demand all of your precious sketches, you might think, *What can I do?* The real question is, *What can't you do?* Creativity can help you out of nearly any situation, and if it can't, well . . . there's always that axe!

Directions:

Pick up the axe from the table. You can swing it at objects in your path to clear them out of the way.

New Objective:

CLEAR A NEW PATH

Clear the boards from the hallway and in front of the doorway to enter the Ritual Room. Step into the transmutation circle to trigger the next story event, and the end of Chapter 1.

CHAPTER TWO

"THE OLD SONG"

Recording Studio

Music Writers' Room

Pool Room

Music Department Entrance

Infirmary

Directions:

After colliding with the transmutation circle, you'll wake up on the floor. Grab the axe and clear the door in front of you. Walking through, you'll come to a large room lit with candles and an audio log from Sammy Lawrence.

Voice of
SAMMY LAWRENCE

He appears from the shadows to rain his sweet blessings upon me. The figure of ink that shines in the darkness. I see you, my savior. I pray you hear me.

Those old songs, I still sing them. For I know you are coming to save me. And I will be swept into your final loving embrace.

But, love requires sacrifice. Can I get an amen?

Directions:

Walking through the flooded hallway, you'll see an inky figure—Sammy Lawrence—carrying a Bendy cutout. He disappears into the wall, but you can still hear him if you approach the wall and listen closely. He says, "Sheep, sheep, it's time for sleep. In the morning, you may wake, or in the morning, you'll be dead."

Continue to the right to find a closed gate that you'll need to power to continue.

New Objective:

REDIRECT POWER TO THE GATE

You'll find the first switch to the left of the "Bendy in Train Trouble" poster. The second switch is in an alcove to the right of two coffins leaning against a wall. The third switch is at the end of the ink-flooded hallway. You'll need to eat a few cans of Bacon Soup to clear the way to the switch beneath them.

UNDEFEATABLE BENDY

If you use your axe to destroy the Bendy cardboard cutouts that appear over a transmutation circle, you'll find they have reappeared, entirely intact, when you next return to the same spot.

New Objective:

RAISE THE GATE

After raising the gate, clear the doorway to enter the Music Department.

The Music Department

At Joey Drew Studios, it takes all kinds of talent to create a masterpiece, from character artists to animators to voice actors to the very theaters that bring our cartoons to the masses. And a vital part of every cartoon is the music.

Here in the Music Department you'll find our state-of-the-art recording studio. Each month our music director, Sammy Lawrence, brings the best musicians from around the country to our studio to record the music and sound effects that underpin every Joey Drew cartoon. A projector above the recording hall helps the orchestra and voice actors stay in sync and make adjustments to the music as they perform. Mr. Lawrence himself composes each song and oversees its recording to ensure it is expertly produced from start to finish.

JOEY DREW STUDIOS

Voice of
SAMMY LAWRENCE

So first, Joey installs this Ink Machine over our heads. Then it begins to leak. Three times last month, we couldn't even get out of our department because the ink had flooded the stairwell.

Joey's solution? An ink pump to drain it periodically. Now I have this ugly pump switch right in my office. People in and out all day.

Thanks, Joey. Just what I needed. More distractions. These stupid cartoon songs don't write themselves, you know.

New Objective:
DRAIN THE STAIRWELL

Entering the Music Department, you'll find that the stairwell to the exit is flooded. You'll need to find a way to drain it. Flip the power switch in the stairwell to turn on the lights.

After returning from the stairwell, you'll be attacked by seven Searchers. These humanoid blobs emerge from ink puddles or leaks in the ink pipes. Two hits with an axe can dispatch a Searcher, or one hit directly to the head. Taking five hits from a Searcher will land you at a respawn point. These enemies may seem like small fries, but if they set upon you in a pack, they can take you down quickly. Try funneling them through a doorway and walking backward as you swing the axe.

Recreation

You've no doubt heard the old adage about "all work and no play." While our company doesn't necessarily condone that philosophy, we can see the value in allowing our employees the chance to blow off steam from time to time. For this reason, various departments are equipped with recreational activities, including darts or billiards. These activities are off-limits to employees and will be locked during work hours, but are available during federally required meal breaks.

Of course, don't expect any kind of reward for obtaining a bull's-eye or sinking a "trick shot" at pool. Time is money, after all.

Directions:
Defeating the Searchers in the Music Department opens a secret pool room to the right of the "Sent from Above" poster. You can play by clicking on the cue ball, which appears to be an eye.

Directions:

A gate to the left of the main area will open, leading you to a hallway containing Sammy Lawrence's office. You'll see a massive ink leak spilling out over the door and an audio log from Wally Franks. You'll find his missing keys in one of the trash bins located throughout the area.

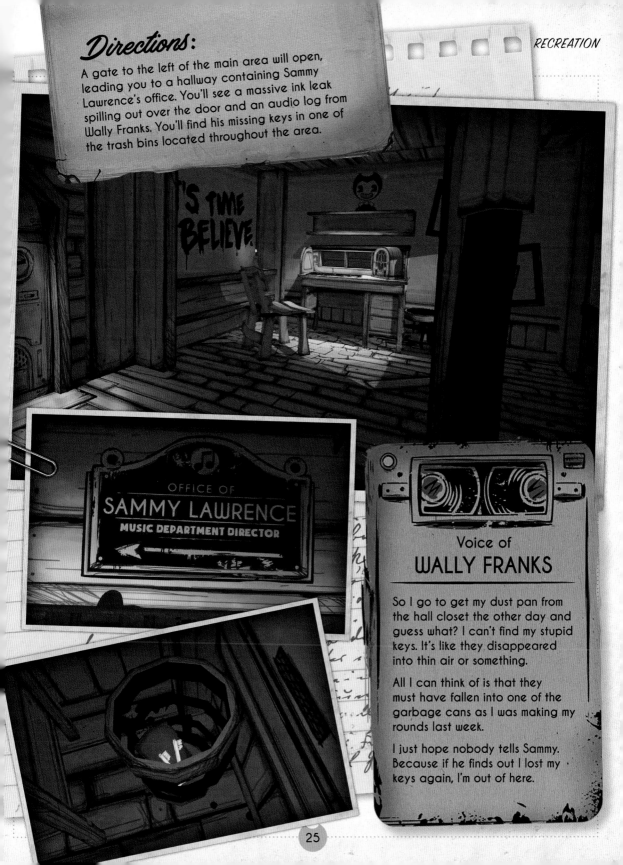

OFFICE OF
SAMMY LAWRENCE
MUSIC DEPARTMENT DIRECTOR

Voice of
WALLY FRANKS

So I go to get my dust pan from the hall closet the other day and guess what? I can't find my stupid keys. It's like they disappeared into thin air or something.

All I can think of is that they must have fallen into one of the garbage cans as I was making my rounds last week.

I just hope nobody tells Sammy. Because if he finds out I lost my keys again, I'm out of here.

Storage Closets

Y ou'll find storage closets throughout Joey Drew Studios. These closets are generally owned by different departments and are often used for supplies. If you belong to a department that has access to a closet, you can ask your manager for keys to it; otherwise most closets usually remain locked to deter thieves or inefficiency.

Some closets belong to the maintenance staff, headed by the aforementioned Wally Franks. Mr. Franks does his best to keep our sprawling studio sparkling clean with the supplies he's budgeted, so please refrain from taking any items from his janitorial closets.

Directions:

Taking the keys back to the right of Sammy's office, you'll find a door labeled "Closet" that will now be unlocked. Inside is another audio log and a new objective.

New Objective:

FIND SAMMY'S SANCTUARY

Voice of
SAMMY LAWRENCE

Every artistic person needs a sanctuary. Joey Drew has his and I have mine. To enter, you need only know my favorite song.

Directions:

Before completing this section, you may want to check out the "Strike Up the Band" achievement on page 35. Note that Sammy's favorite song changes with each game, so you will likely have a different instrument or instrument order.

Return to the area you first entered, and walk up the stairs to the right. You'll find an audio log from Norman Polk as well as a projector you can turn on. Activate the projector, then go downstairs to the recording studio. Interact with the instruments in Sammy's song in the correct order to open his sanctuary.

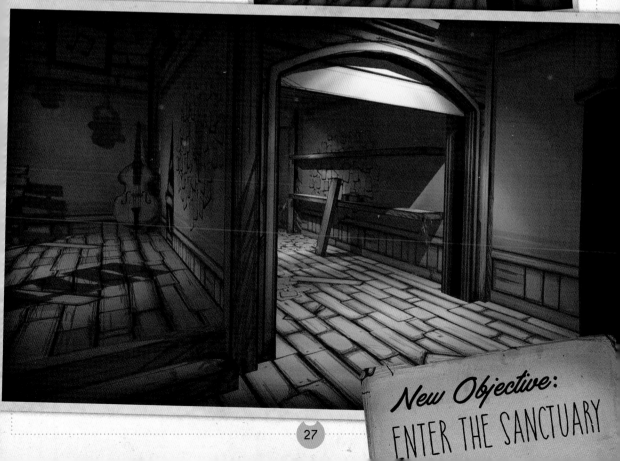

New Objective:
ENTER THE SANCTUARY

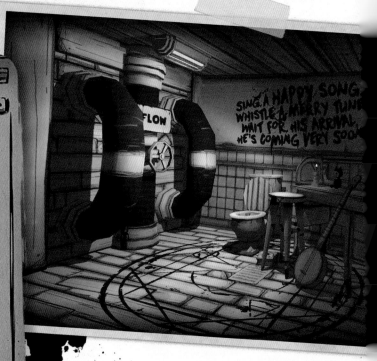

Voice of
NORMAN POLK

Every day, the same strange thing happens. I'll be up here in my booth, the band will be swinging, and suddenly Sammy Lawrence just comes marching in and shuts the whole thing down. Tells us all to wait in the hall.

Then I hear him. He starts up my projector, and he dashes from the projector booth and down to the recording studio like the little devil himself was chasing behind.

Few seconds later, the projector turns off. But Sammy, he doesn't come out for a long time. This man is weird. Crazy weird.

I have half a mind to talk to Mister Drew about all this. But then again, I have to admit, Mister Drew has his own peculiarities.

SING A HAPPY SONG
WHISTLE A MERRY TUNE
WAIT FOR HIS ARRIVAL,
HE'S COMING VERY SOON

Directions:

The gate to the left of the recording booth will rise, granting you access to Sammy's sanctuary. Inside you'll find a valve to adjust the ink pressure. Turn the valve and proceed back out to the recording studio. You'll catch a glimpse of Sammy himself, watching you, from a balcony to the left of the projector booth.

As he watches, seven Searchers will attack you on your way to the door. If possible, try herding them in a row as you back into Sammy's sanctuary, so as not to become overwhelmed.

JOEY DREW STUDIOS

From: Joey Drew

Memo to Staff Regarding New Initiatives

I'm excited to reveal that Joey Drew Studios will be embarking on a new initiative that's sure to take our studio straight to the top!

All staff and talent are asked to gather in the main lobby at 4:30 PM this Friday to meet Alice Angel, the newest friend of Bendy and Boris the Wolf. Refreshments will be served, along with the chance to meet the voice of Alice herself, Susie Campbell. Don't be late!

Alice Angel

Voice of
SUSIE CAMPBELL

It may only be my second month working for Joey Drew, but I can already tell I'm going to love it here!

People really seem to enjoy my Alice Angel voice. Sammy says she may be as popular as Bendy someday.

These past few weeks I have voiced everything, from talking chairs to dancing chickens. But this is the first character I have really felt a connection with. Like she's part of me.

Alice and I, we are going places.

Medical Needs

FEELING SICK?
WOKE UP WITH AN ACHING BACK?
SLIPPED ON A PUDDLE OF INK?

There's no need to recuperate at home—come visit the Infirmary! Our friendly medical staff is on call several hours each week to tend to your needs. Full-time staff members with **GENUINE ILLNESS OR INJURY** are encouraged to check in at the Infirmary for rest and care. The Infirmary's trained staff will have you up, running, and back to your desk in no time, to ensure your work remains in tip-top shape! If you find that staff is unavailable at the time of your visit, feel free to help yourself to our assortment of first-aid supplies before returning to your desk to finish out the workday.

E
F P   1
HCA   2
PMFYC   3
EDFPZDT   4
ZVBXRPL   5
GBRUOCZ   6
                                      7

NOTICE:

ANYONE FOUND FAKING
ILLNESS WILL BE DOCKED
A FULL WEEK'S WAGES.

NOT SICK. NOT PAID.

PLEASE WAIT

New Objective:

FIND THE SECOND VALVE

You'll find the second valve downstairs in the Infirmary, but the valve itself is missing. You'll need to travel down Utility Shaft 9 to find it. After dispensing with the Searcher in the Infirmary, pull the lever to restore power to the utility shaft and head downstairs.

At the bottom of the stairs, you can spot Sammy's shadow through the grating to your left. Turning right, sliding doors will open, revealing an ink-filled tunnel. Turn left at the end of the tunnel to encounter an ink creature wearing a hat, Swollen Jack. Jack will disappear when you approach him.

Clear the boards overhead with the axe and continue down the tunnel. To your right is an alcove with an audio log from Jack Fain.

Voice of
JACK FAIN

I love the quiet, and that's hard to come by these busy times.

And yeah sure it may stink to high heaven down here. But it's just perfect for an old lyricist like me. Sammy's songs always got some bounce, but if I didn't get away once in a while, they'd never have any words to go with them.

So I'll keep my mind a-singin' and my nose closed.

From: Thomas Connor

Memo to Staff Regarding Utility Shafts

To All Concerned.

We know that the noise from the Ink Machine and the new plumbing has made it hard for you all to get your work done, but just a quick reminder that the utility shafts scattered throughout the building are off-limits. It's really not safe for folks to be down there. If a pipe burst, well—you could find yourself in a sticky spot real fast. We've taken the liberty of boarding off some of them for your own protection. Just stay out of there, okay?

SING
WITH
ME

New Objective:

SWOLLEN JACK

Follow the tunnel until you come to an open boiler room, with Swollen Jack in the back, holding the valve you need. Jack won't attack you and will likely disappear before you can attack him. Even if you do manage a hit, he won't take damage; you will need to outsmart him to obtain the valve. The lever to your left will raise a platform containing a box, while the lever on your right will drop it suddenly. Corral Swollen Jack underneath the platform, then pull the lever to the right to squash him. He'll drop your valve in the process.

Once you grab the valve, return to the Infirmary to restore it to the pipe and close the valve. On the way, you'll notice Sammy's shadow is no longer visible from behind the grating.

New Objective:

RETURN TO SAMMY'S OFFICE

OVERACHIEVER!

A few achievements will be given to you through the natural course of the story:

MY FAVORITE SONG: Solve the music puzzle to open the way to Sammy's sanctuary.

A SPECIAL HAT: Run into Jack Fain.

THE BELIEVER: Survive being chased by Bendy.

But before you head to Sammy's office to finish *Chapter 2: "The Old Song,"* be sure to check the following items off your to-do list:

COAST TO COAST: Turn on the radio, which you'll find in Sammy's office.

JOHNNY'S BROKEN HEART: Head down the hallway that leads to Sammy's office. The first door on your right opens into a room with a pipe organ. Play the organ five times, waiting after each time to hear a moaning voice, and you will unlock this achievement.

STRIKE UP THE BAND: For this achievement, you'll need to travel from the booth to the stage. Repeat this ten times, noting that a new Bendy cutout appears onstage with each trip (up to nine Bendys in all). When you successfully open the sanctuary, all the Bendys will appear up in the loft where you saw Sammy lurking.

MAN BEHIND THE CURTAIN: Visit theMeatly. Go down the hallway toward Sammy's office and enter the second door on the right. Walk through the "Sheep Songs" poster to the right of the first desk.

OLD PROBLEMS: Listen to all the audio logs in this chapter. There are seven:
- Three from Sammy Lawrence: One before the ink-flooded hallway, one when you enter the Music Department, and one in the supply closet.
- One from Wally Franks outside Sammy's office.
- One from Susie Campbell by the piano in the recording studio.
- One from Norman Polk in the projector booth above the recording studio.
- One from Jack Fain in Utility Shaft 9.

CANADIAN BACON: Collect all the Bacon Soup in this chapter (see page 36).

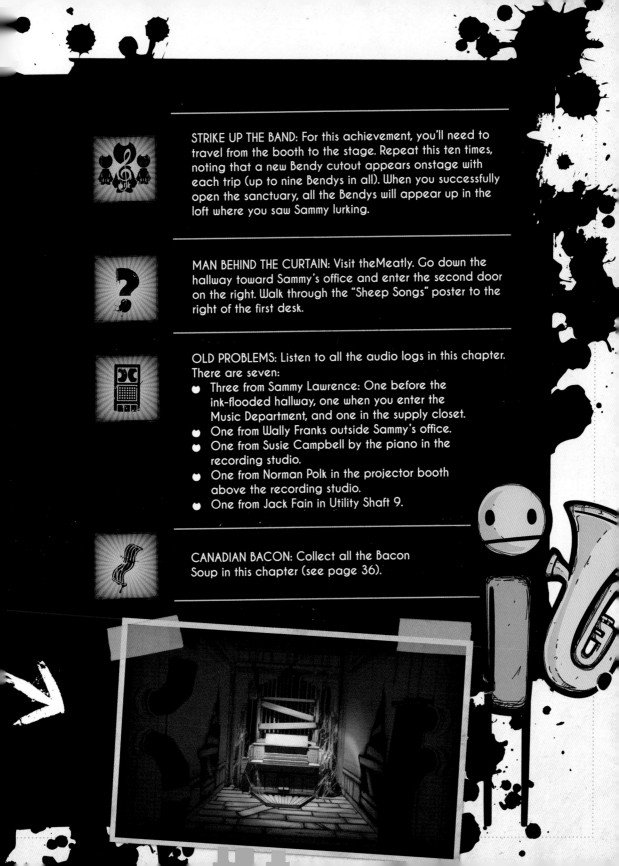

STUDIO LAYOUT

CANADIAN BACON

There are thirty-one cans of Bacon Soup scattered throughout the studio in Chapter 2. Be sure to get them all for the "Canadian Bacon" achievement.

- Three cans, in the shelving underneath the "He will set us free" writing on the wall.
- Twenty cans, in the shelves near the third switch.
- One can, on the first desk you see when you walk into the office.
- Four cans, in the supply closet outside of Sammy's office.
- One can, on Jack Fain's piano down Utility Shaft 9.

After Sammy knocks you out . . .

- One can, when you're free from Sammy, walk straight, in front of the loose boards, then to the right. You'll find a Bendy statue, and one can to the right of its feet, beside a barrel.
- One can, after escaping Bendy, on top of a barrel in front of a shelf of Bendy toys.

Briar Label Bacon Soup

By now, we're sure you're wondering, *What's with all the soup?*

As part of Bendy's licensing agreement with Briar Label Bacon Soup, the Briar Label Company has stocked Joey Drew Studios from roof to sub-sub-sub-sub-basement with free soup as a thank-you. Made from a traditional family recipe, Briar Label Bacon Soup tastes just like the home-kitchen cooking that Mom used to make. Rather than going out for lunch, please indulge in a free meal on us while you work at your desk—forks are available upon request.

After eating, please leave your dirty bowls in the dedicated shelving in the stairwell for Wally Franks. And don't forget to rinse and deposit your tin cans in salvage bins to help the war effort!

JUST THE WAY THE LITTLE DEVIL LIKES IT.

New Objective:

THE MINER SEARCHER

Backtrack to the Ritual Room with the transmutation circle (where you started Chapter 2) to unlock a secret boss. You'll need to battle several new Searchers as you backtrack. From the transmutation circle, a new boss forms—an ink creature wearing a hard hat. This Miner Searcher does a significant amount of damage if it hits you, so be careful. You can do several things with this creature:

- You can kill this boss with four swings of your axe, but doing so will result in nothing.

- Lead it back to the boiler room where you squashed Swollen Jack. Squash this creature in the same manner to trigger a creepy noise and a glitching screen. You'll hear the rumbling noise repeat throughout the level. This action is required to obtain the Scythe (see page 122).

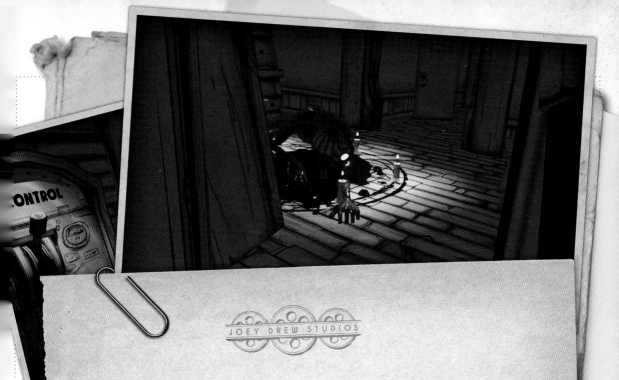

JOEY DREW STUDIOS

From: Sammy Lawrence

To: All Staff Regarding the Music Department

Musical instruments aren't just for fun. We do serious work here at the Music Department. While I know it may be tempting, please refrain from playing musical instruments in our corridors.

Just last week I had to rerecord a song because someone was plucking a banjo just outside the recording studio. Whoever it was, please stop it. And please, everyone, stop making so much noise in general. No more loud shoes, whistling, humming, or gum chewing by the Music Department.

You have been warned.

Directions:

Back upstairs, the ink gushing over Sammy's office door has stopped, and you'll be able to get inside. Flip the "Pump Control" switch to drain the stairwell. Before you go, you can check out a blueprint of the Ink Machine on Sammy's desk.

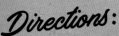

New Objective:
TAKE THE STAIRS

When you reach the end of the hall, Sammy will knock you out and drag you away. When you come to, Sammy has tied you up, prepared to offer you up to Bendy.

Directions:

Sammy then leaves the room to summon Ink Bendy. As you struggle to get free, you can hear Ink Bendy turn on Sammy, attacking him. A pool of ink will leak out from under the door Sammy went through, and you're able to free yourself.

New Objective:
ESCAPE BENDY

Dispatch the five Searchers in the room and head through the newly opened gate. Break the boards in the hallway to clear a path. In the first alcove to your right, you'll be able to get a peek at the Ink Machine lowering from the upper level. After chopping up the last board in the hallway, your axe will break.

Ink Bendy will appear in the ink-flooded room at the end of the hall, and you'll have to escape him. More and more ink will pool on the walls and floor as Ink Bendy gets closer, so be sure to stay ahead of him. Eventually you'll get to a room and the door will lock behind you. Continue on to encounter Boris the Wolf.

After your axe breaks, linger in the hallway for a minute just outside the ink-flooded room where Ink Bendy appears. If you stay for long enough, you'll be able to hear Bendy's whistle, which you also heard in the Theater in Chapter 1.

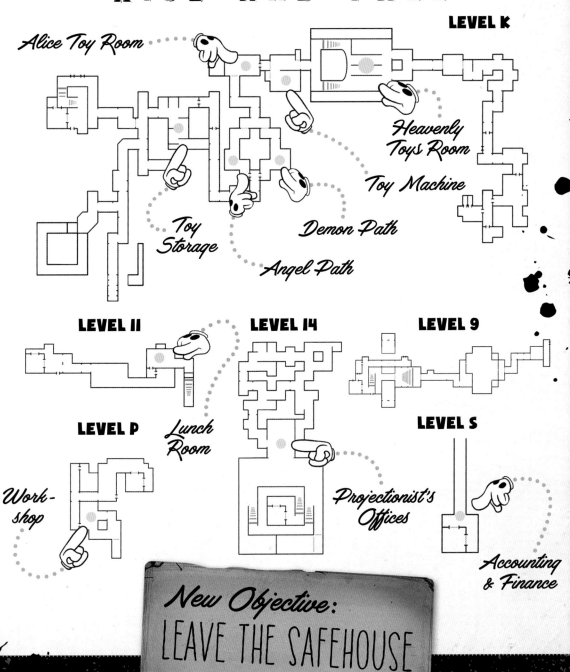

FUN FACT!
The name "Boris" comes from the extinct Bulgar language, where it meant "Wolf," and Boris is a Wolf!

Boris the Wolf

Every animated character needs a best pal, and Bendy has one in Boris the Wolf! Boris isn't quite as bright as Bendy, so he often ends up with the short end of the stick in Bendy's schemes. Through it all, Boris stays loyal to his friends, so long as they don't come between him and his lunch!

From Joey Drew

When we first had the idea for Bendy, we were so excited, but our little devil got bored quickly. What's the point of a laugh if you can't share it with your pals? We created Boris the Wolf mainly to keep things interesting, but he quickly evolved into one of our company's favorite characters. I mean, can you imagine the joy of wearing overalls every day? Our animators should know, though, that there's a lot more to Boris than meets the eye. Is he perhaps a wolf in sheep's clothing after all? Maybe you'll tell us!

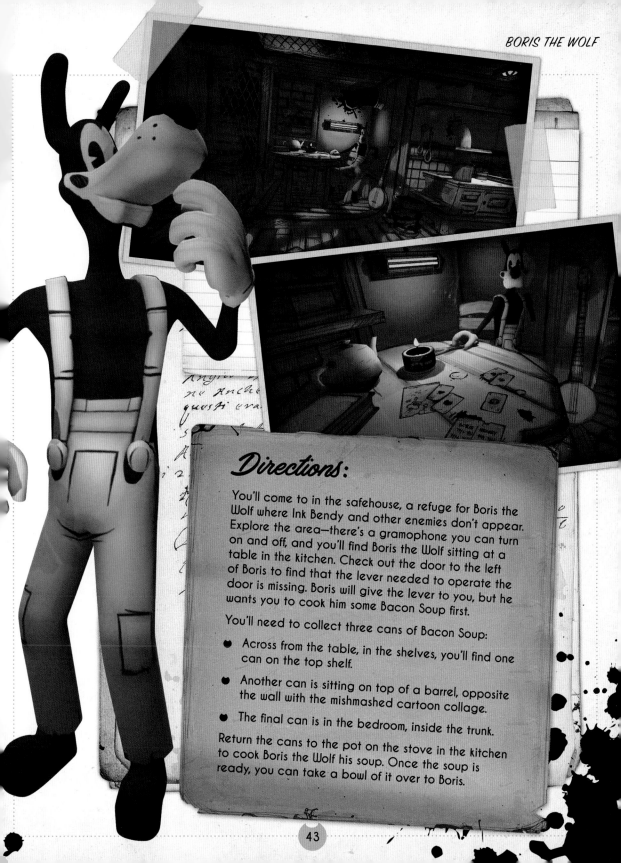

Directions:

You'll come to in the safehouse, a refuge for Boris the Wolf where Ink Bendy and other enemies don't appear. Explore the area—there's a gramophone you can turn on and off, and you'll find Boris the Wolf sitting at a table in the kitchen. Check out the door to the left of Boris to find that the lever needed to operate the door is missing. Boris will give the lever to you, but he wants you to cook him some Bacon Soup first.

You'll need to collect three cans of Bacon Soup:

- Across from the table, in the shelves, you'll find one can on the top shelf.

- Another can is sitting on top of a barrel, opposite the wall with the mishmashed cartoon collage.

- The final can is in the bedroom, inside the trunk.

Return the cans to the pot on the stove in the kitchen to cook Boris the Wolf his soup. Once the soup is ready, you can take a bowl of it over to Boris.

New Objective:
FIND THE EXIT

As soon as Boris is satisfied, he'll take out a box containing the lever you'll need. Place the lever handle on the mechanism to the left of the door and pull it to open. Boris will hop up from the table to leave. You won't be able to return to the safehouse once you exit it, so proceed with caution.

New Objective:
ENTER THE DARKNESS

Wander ahead with Boris until you come to a long, dark hallway. You'll need to retrieve the flashlight from a desk to the right before entering the darkness.

In the dark corridor, you'll see moving gears, ink jars, and splattering ink. Boris will get scared and stop moving, so keep the light near him! Continue on until you reach a room that appears to be a dead end, where it's a little brighter. Once you reach this room, the door will close behind you.

From here, you'll need to give Boris your flashlight so he can crawl through the vents to open the door. After a minute or so, the doors will slide open, clearing your way toward the Heavenly Toys Room.

GIVE A WOLF A BONE
Before you leave the safehouse, check out this fun Easter egg: return to the bedroom, where you'll find a bone to the left of the trunk. You can give it to Boris, who will gnaw on it throughout the chapter. This will also earn you the "Knick-Knack Paddywhack" achievement.

New Objective:
FIND THE EXIT

New Objective:
FIX THE TOY MACHINE

As you head into the Heavenly Toys Room, you can faintly hear someone humming. Head up the steps and into the workshop. The toy machine in the workshop is broken, and you'll need to fix it if you want to clear a path to access the rooms beyond.

Go back into the Heavenly Toys Room and find the lever by the staircase. Once there, pull it. Next you'll need to unclog the belt wheels by collecting the toys that are stuck in them. You'll need to collect four plush toys before continuing on.

INK BLOB
If you're planning to complete the "Blazing Metal" achievement, squeeze into the little alcove where Shawn Flynn's audio log is. Interact with the ink blob on the desk until it takes the shape of a tiny Ink Machine. If you're interested in the Lever Challenge, morph the ink blob into Boris.

Voice of
SHAWN FLYNN

I don't be seein' what the big deal is.

So what if I went and painted some of those Bendy dolls with a crooked smile?

That's sure no reason for Mister Drew to be flyin' off the handle at me. And if he really wants to be so helpful, he could be tellin' me what I'm to be doin' with this warehouse I got full of that angel whatchamacallit. Not a scrap of that mess be a-sellin'! Probably have to melt it all down to be rid of it all.

New Objective:
TURN ON THE TOY MACHINE

Now you'll need to turn the machine on. On the right side of the room, pull the lever that's located between two of the belt wheels. Several shelves of toys will slide away, revealing an unlocked door.

THE ERIE I

12 September 1933

LATE C

JOEY DI
DEBUTS

New York, NY—Joining the ranks of beloved cartoon characters Bendy and Boris the Wolf is Alice Angel, the newest character at Joey Drew Studios.

"It has always been part of our plan to bring a dynamic, strong, and intelligent character like Alice to the table," said Joey Drew, president and founder of the company. "Alice isn't your typical girl next door. She's a character with charm, but brains too. When Bendy is getting up to something, Alice is there to throw a wrench into his schemes."

As the first female character for Joey Drew Studios, Alice Angel certainly

AILY TIMES

TION

TWO CENTS

EW STUDIOS
ALICE ANGEL

has a lot to live up to. We asked Joey what kind of gal Alice Angel will be.

"What kind of gal? Well, she's quite a gal," said Joey Drew with a wry smile. "She sings; she dances. We think Alice's fiery, sharp character will really resonate with Bendy fans, and we're excited to introduce her to our animation cartoons and merchandise."

Alice Angel merchandise will be available next year through Joey Drew Studios' upcoming toy line, Heavenly Toys. She will be voiced by actress Susie Campbell.

ALICE ANGEL'S CHAMBER

Through the unblocked door you will enter a new room—Alice Angel's chamber. The lights will go out, and several TV screens will flicker to life, singing Alice's theme song. Through the glass window straight ahead, you'll meet the twisted Alice Angel for the first time. She will scream, break the glass, and escape into the room.

SHE'S QUITE A GAL!

Voice of
JOEY DREW

There's nothing wrong with dreaming. Wishing for the impossible is just human nature. That's how I got started. Just a pencil and a dream. We all want everything without even having to lift a finger.

They say you just have to believe.

Belief can make you succeed. Belief can make you rich. Belief can make you powerful.

Why, with enough belief, you can even cheat death itself.

Now that . . . is a beautiful, and positively silly thought.

ALICE ANGEL

I'm the cutest little angel, sent from above, and I know just how to swing.

I got a bright little halo, and I'm filled with love . . .

I'm Alice Angel!

I'm the hit of the party, I'm the belle of the ball, I'm the toast of every town.

Just one little dance, and I know you'll fall . . .

I'm Alice Angel!

I ain't no flapper, I'm a classy dish, and boy, can this girl sing.

This gal can grant your every wish . . .

I'm Alice Angel!

New Objective:
FIND A NEW EXIT

When the lights come back on, turn to your left to walk through several narrow corridors until you come to a fork in the path and a sign. You can choose one of two routes: The "Demon" route, and the "Angel" route. Taking each path is an achievement, but if you're looking to accomplish the "Blazing Metal" achievement, you'll need to take the Demon path. Take the Angel path if you'd like to complete the Lever Challenge.

THE ANGEL
Choose the right side and you'll find a brightly lit room with a couch and an audio recording from Susie Campbell.

THE DEMON
ANGEL

THE DEMON
Veer to the left and you'll walk through the Demon route, which is flooded with ink. Here you will encounter a new audio recording from Joey Drew.

Voice of
SUSIE CAMPBELL

Everything feels like it's coming apart.

When I walked into the recording booth today, Sammy was there with that . . . Allison.

Apparently, I didn't get the memo. Alice Angel will now be voiced by Miss Allison Pendle.

A part of me died when he said that.

There's gotta be a way to fix this!

From: Joey Drew

To: All Staff

Please give a warm welcome to Allison Pendle, Joey Drew Studios' newest employee. Allison is a talented voice actress with lots of dreams. In her spare time, she loves to cook and invent recipes. I know that as soon as you meet her, you'll be taken with her beautiful voice and charm. She's so interesting, so . . . different. I have to say, I'm an instant fan.

Effective immediately, Allison will be the new voice of Alice Angel. We believe this restructure in voice talent will lead to a more cohesive character list—and more success for our dreams.

Allison will meet with Sammy Lawrence after lunch to discuss rerecording Alice Angel's dialogue. Then I will bring her around to meet everyone.

Distribute immediately to all employees except for Susie Campbell.

Directions:

Press on, and you'll get a Bendy cutout jump scare, courtesy of Boris. Boris has returned with a Gent pipe you can use to arm yourself.

New Objective:
ARM YOURSELF

Through the door you'll find an ink-flooded room with toys, clocks, and stuffed animals based on the studio's animated characters. Boris will lead you to a Bendy statue; here, you'll find the first of two switches.

BENDY IN

15 5 CENTS

"THE BUTCHER GANG"

PRESENTED IN SILLYVISION

New Objective:
OPEN THE STORAGE EXIT

Turn around and follow the cables to the second switch, which appears to the left of a poster for the Butcher Gang. The poster will break open to reveal a Piper, the twisted version of cartoon Charley from the Butcher Gang. You will need to hit this enemy roughly six times in order to defeat him. Only then will the lever become available to you.

Before flipping the lever, explore the area. Coming back toward Boris, the first corridor on the left will lead you to several discoveries. There's an audio log from Wally Franks and Thomas Connor sitting in the hallway. The first room on the right will give you a view of the Ink Machine being lowered once again.

New Objective:
FIND A NEW EXIT

After you're done exploring, return and flip the lever, following Boris through to the new exit. You'll come out into an open area with a marking for Level K and a large elevator.

Upon entering the elevator, you and Boris will hear Alice Angel's voice as you descend lower and lower. The elevator will bring you to Level 9 of the studio, where Alice resides.

Voice of
WALLY and THOMAS

Wally: Alright, let's go over this again. If the pressure goes over 45, I screw the safety bolt in tighter, right?

Thomas: No! For the last time, you do that, you'll blow every pipe in this place! If it reaches 45, you unhook the safety switch.

Wally: You sure? You know, this sounds harder than comparing ear wax to bee's wax!

Thomas: Look, it's not that difficult! Just keep an eye on the gauge!

Wally: Look pal, if you think I'm doing my job AND yours, I'm outta here!

Voice of
THOMAS CONNOR

These blasted elevators . . . sometimes they open, sometimes they don't . . . sometimes they come . . . sometimes they keep on going to hell and back.

I keep telling these people, if Mister Joey Drew keeps cutting corners like this, someone's sure to end up falling to their death. And it sure ain't gonna be me.

I'm taking the stairs.

New Objective:
DATE WITH AN ANGEL

Exit the elevator and head down a flight of stairs to encounter an audio log from Thomas Connor.

Directions:

Descend the set of stairs in front of you, then head across the bridge to another flight of stairs, this time leading up to a closed doorway with Alice Angel's face and slogan atop it. As you near it with Boris, the doors will slide open. Boris will run through the narrow hallway and you will follow him, passing a cardboard cutout of Alice as you go.

In the new room, you'll find multiple clones of Boris and Charley, each one sacrificed to make Alice beautiful and more "perfect." As you explore the room, you'll find an audio log from Susie Campbell.

Continue on through the corridors until you come upon twisted Alice, who will tell you about how she became an "angel," as she describes it. Alice says she will let you leave if you perform various errands for her.

"DO YOU KNOW WHAT IT'S LIKE? LIVING IN THE DARK PUDDLES?
• IT'S A BUZZING, SCREAMING WELL
• OF VOICES! BITS OF YOUR MIND, SWIMMING... LIKE... FISH IN A BOWL! THE FIRST TIME I WAS BORN FROM ITS INKY WOMB, I WAS A WIGGLING, PUSSING, SHAPELESS SLUG. THE SECOND TIME... WELL... IT MADE ME AN ANGEL! I WILL NOT LET THE DEMON TOUCH ME AGAIN I'M SO CLOSE NOW. SO. ALMOST PERFECT."

New Objective:
DO THE ANGEL'S BIDDING

Voice of
SUSIE CAMPBELL

Who would have thought? Me having lunch with Joey Drew! Apparently times are tougher than I thought.

For a moment there, I thought I'd be stuck with the check. But I gotta say, he wasn't at all what I expected. Quite the charmer. He even called me Alice. I liked it!

Joe's Fine Dining

555 Christopher Street, New York, NY

For the finest quality at reasonable prices, Joe's Fine Dining cannot be beat!

NO REFUNDS ACCEPTED

2	Bacon Soup
1	Linguini Alfredo
1	Filet Mignon
1	Iced Tea
1	Lemonade
1	Strawberry Cheesecake

Joe's Fine Dining

555 Christopher Street, New York, NY

For the finest quality at reasonable prices, Joe's Fine Dining cannot be beat!

NO REFUNDS ACCEPTED

2	Bacon Soup
1	Linguini Alfredo
1	Filet Mignon
1	Iced Tea
1	Lemonade
1	Strawberry Cheesecake

Welcome lunch for Susie Campbell. Quite the charmer.

New Objective: COLLECT THREE GEARS

New Objective: TAKE THE WRENCH

After returning to the elevator, trade your Gent pipe for a wrench, which you can collect from the revolving cupboard to the left of the "She's quite a gal!" sliding doors. Enter the elevator and travel back to Level K to collect three gears for Alice's machines. From the elevator, take the stairs up and head through the corridor.

1. You'll likely find the first gear in the hands of a Piper, the twisted version of Charley from the Butcher Gang. Defeat him to obtain it.

2. As you backtrack into the storage area, you'll see maintenance panels on the walls, which will contain the remaining gears. Many of these panels are empty, but the second gear can be found by opening the panel on the left side of the storage room, between the two shelves of toys.

3. The final gear can be found at the end of the long hallway on the right side of the storage room. You will have to defeat a Searcher to access it.

New Objective: RETURN TO THE ANGEL

Return to Alice on Level 9, and deposit the gears into the drop box to the right of the sliding doors.

New Objective: TAKE THE INK SYRINGE

INK BENDY

Throughout this chapter, you may be set upon by Ink Bendy. You'll be able to see him approach by the weblike lines of ink that appear over the floor and grow darker the closer Ink Bendy gets. When you see him approach, make your way to a Little Miracle Station and get inside. Ink Bendy cannot attack you in here; wait until the lines of ink disappear before exiting.

New Objective:
COLLECT THREE EXTRA THICK INK

Take the Ink Syringe Alice will provide you and head up to Level 11, and walk straight out of the elevators down the hallway, fighting the Searchers along the way.

1. Fight the Fisher, the corrupted version of Barley from the Butcher Gang, wandering around the level. After defeating him, a pulsing glob of ink will appear on the ground, which you can collect.

2. Continue straight back into an open room with a stream of ink flowing toward a Little Miracle Station. Outside the station, a Swollen Searcher will form. Defeat it to obtain your second glob of ink.

3. In the corner opposite where you found the first Swollen Searcher, another will form. This Searcher will sometimes disappear and reappear in the back of the room. Defeat it to get the final glob of ink.

In the back of the room with the two Swollen Searchers is a room with a window. Here you'll get your first peek at the Projectionist, whom you'll encounter later in this chapter. An audio log from Wally Franks also appears here.

New Objective:
RETURN TO THE ANGEL

Voice of
WALLY FRANKS

I don't get it.

Everyone's walking around here like grandma just died. Nothing but angry faces everywhere.

These people gotta lighten up. I mean hello! You make cartoons! Your job is to make people laugh.

I'm tellin' ya, if these people don't start crackin' a smile every now and then, I'm outta here.

BEFORE YOU RETURN TO ALICE...

Head into the stairway on Level 11 to find an alcove full of musical instruments. Play the bass, drum, violin, piano, and drum in that order to hear a secret message from Sammy Lawrence.

"WE'VE ALL BEEN WAITING BUT NOW, HE WILL SET... US... FREE..."

Directions:

As before, deposit the extra thick ink into the drop box. Your syringe will disappear and you'll be given a plunger.

New Objective:
TAKE THE PLUNGER

New Objective:
COLLECT THREE VALVE CORES

Take the elevator or stairs to Level P. From the elevator, make a U-turn down a hallway into a large open room. Straight ahead you'll see three glass walls encasing another room.

1. The first valve core is obtained from defeating a Striker, the demented version of Edgar from the Butcher Gang, which should wander up to you.

2. Enter the glass room on the right, which you'll see when walking away from the elevator. Here you'll find three valves below three tubes of ink set into the nonglass wall. Each tube has a dot in the middle. Turn the valves until all the ink levels match the dots. When they do, a door to the left of the valves will open, containing the second valve core.

3. Exit the first glass room and continue straight down the hallway to enter another glass room. Turn right at the "Little Devil Darlin'" poster and make a left, toward a "Hell in a Handbasket" poster. You'll see another set of valves to the right of the poster. Solve this puzzle in the same way to obtain your third valve core.

New Objective:
RETURN TO THE ANGEL

CORPORATION WARRANTY

A SPECIAL PROMISE TO OUR CUSTOMERS

At Gent Corporation, we strive to make the best products possible for our customers. With quality craftsmanship, friendly staff, and expert machinists, we're certain you'll be satisfied with our products and service. If you follow our service manual to the letter and suffer a malfunction with your Gent device, we will be happy to send one of our qualified staff members to assist you, for as long as it takes to make things right.

This warranty is valid for ten years of service, no matter the issue, big or small!

WARRANTY

Directions:

Back on Level 9, leave the valve cores in the drop box to obtain your new tool, the axe.

New Objective:
TAKE THE AXE

New Objective:
DESTROY ALL BENDY CUTOUTS

Return to Level K, where you'll need to destroy all the Bendy cutouts on this level—sixteen in all. To ensure you get all of them, it's easiest to backtrack to the beginning of the level and start there:

- Facing the staircases, there are four Bendy cutouts on the left side of the room.

- There are another four on the right side of the room.

- Heading through Alice Angel's chamber, you'll find one on the path toward the Angel/Demon fork in the path, leaning against a barrel.

- One on the Demon or Angel path (whichever path you took, you'll find one in that room).

- Upon exiting the Demon or Angel path, there's a cutout immediately to your right, leaning against a wall.

- After a series of corridors, you'll find one right outside the door to the storage room.

- There are three in the toy storage room.

- Heading down the stairs toward the elevator, jump over the railing near the landing to destroy the last Bendy cutout to the right of the elevator.

Voice of
GRANT COHEN

They say the real problem with Mister Drew is that he never actually tells us little people anything.

Oh sure, according to him there's always big stuff coming, adventure and fame and the like.

But I'm the guy, see, who has to make sure our budgets don't go all out of whack just 'cause genius upstairs went out and got himself another idea. Speaking of which, and this is top secret, apparently Mister Drew has another large project in mind now ... and it ain't cheap.

BEFORE YOU RETURN THAT AXE . . .

Before you return to Alice on Level 9, exit the elevators on that level and turn to the left to find a boarded-up door under the "Level 9" sign. Hack away the boards and enter the office to find a secret audio log from Joey Drew Studios' Accounting & Finance Department director, Grant Cohen. There is also a spare axe here, hidden between two crates. Do not pick the axe up; wait until after you return Alice's axe to retrieve this one.

New Objective:
RETURN TO THE ANGEL

Directions:

When you return to Alice, she'll have another task for you: Kill the Butcher Gang.

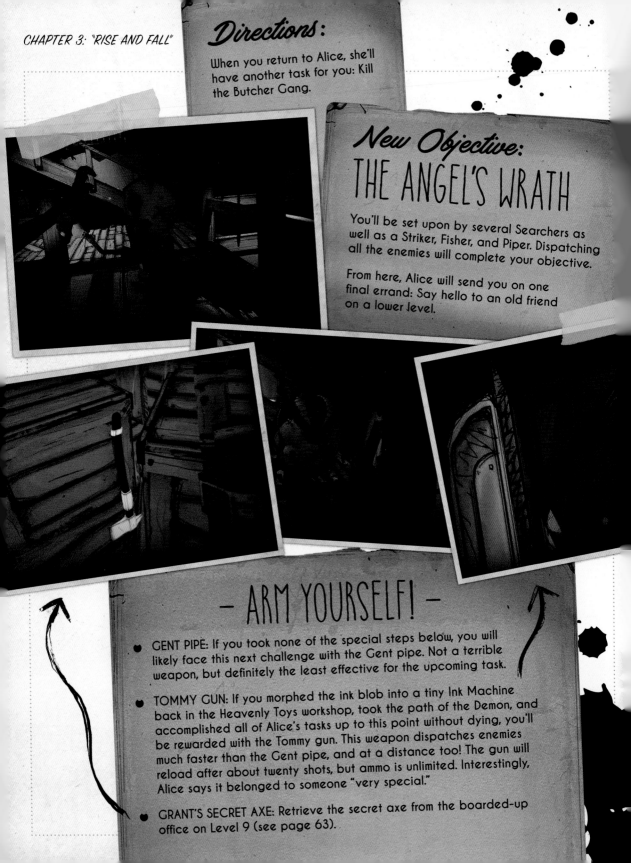

New Objective:
THE ANGEL'S WRATH

You'll be set upon by several Searchers as well as a Striker, Fisher, and Piper. Dispatching all the enemies will complete your objective.

From here, Alice will send you on one final errand: Say hello to an old friend on a lower level.

– ARM YOURSELF! –

- **GENT PIPE:** If you took none of the special steps below, you will likely face this next challenge with the Gent pipe. Not a terrible weapon, but definitely the least effective for the upcoming task.

- **TOMMY GUN:** If you morphed the ink blob into a tiny Ink Machine back in the Heavenly Toys workshop, took the path of the Demon, and accomplished all of Alice's tasks up to this point without dying, you'll be rewarded with the Tommy gun. This weapon dispatches enemies much faster than the Gent pipe, and at a distance too! The gun will reload after about twenty shots, but ammo is unlimited. Interestingly, Alice says it belonged to someone "very special."

- **GRANT'S SECRET AXE:** Retrieve the secret axe from the boarded-up office on Level 9 (see page 63).

New Objective:
TAKE THE TOMMY GUN

— LEVER CHALLENGE —

If you morphed the ink blob in the Heavenly Toys workshop into Boris, took the path of the Angel, and unblocked the secret office with Grant Cohen's audio log, a special challenge will unlock for you. After dispatching the Butcher Gang and retrieving the secret axe, return to the Toy Workshop. You'll see a wall that's been boarded up from floor to ceiling, to the left of a "Work Hard, Work Happy" sign. Hack away the boards to reveal three levers, labeled "For service, please pull lever."

● Pulling the first lever summons a horde of Searchers.

● Pulling the second lever summons multiple Butcher Gangs.

● Pulling the third lever summons a giant Searcher Boss.

OVERACHIEVER!

A few achievements will be given to you through the natural course of the story:

 DARKER PLACES: Survive the Inky Abyss (where the Projectionist lurks).

 FRONT LINES: Survive the Butcher Gang's attack.

 THE PATH OF THE DEMON: Choose the way of Bendy.

 ANGER MANAGEMENT: Destroy all Bendy cutouts in Chapter 3.

 THE PATH OF THE ANGEL: Choose the way of Alice.

 FEELING THE PRESSURE: Solve all valve panel puzzles.

 ULTIMATE STOMACHACHE: Hunt down all Swollen Searchers.

 SPARE PARTS: Find all of Alice Angel's gears.

WANDERING IS A TERRIBLE SIN.

SOME ADDITIONAL EASTER EGGS!

- Hackers looking to peer behind some of the walled-off areas of this and other chapters have been met with this terrifying Bendy.

- In the stairwell directly above the sunken room, you'll see a boarded-off area above the wall. Between the boards you can see what appears to be a second Ink Machine that looks different from the main story version.

But before you return to Alice to finish *Chapter 3: Rise and Fall*, be sure to check the following items off your to-do list:

KNICK-KNACK PADDYWHACK: Get the poor doggie a bone (see page 44).

BLAZING METAL: Unleash the Tommy gun (see page 62).

TURN IT UP: Turn on the radio in Chapter 3, which appears in the stairwell on Level 11, near all the musical instruments.

NORMAN'S FATE: Bring down the Projectionist (see page 68).

INNER CHILD: Play with twenty-five Bendy dolls. You need only interact with the dolls—they'll make a squeaking sound.

BRING HOME THE BACON: Collect all Bacon Soup in Chapter 3 (see page 67).

LONG FORGOTTEN SELF: Listen to Henry's audio log (see page 69).

HEARING VOICES: Listen to all the audio logs in Chapter 3 (see page 67).

TEA TIME: Kick back with theMeatly. Head to Level P. In the small workshop room, to the right of the final valve puzzle you solved is a "Sheep Songs" poster. Walk through the wall to find theMeatly.

STUDIO LAYOUT

LEVEL K

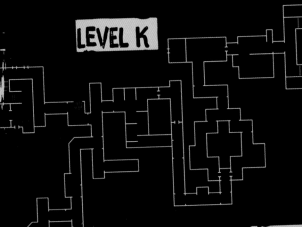

LEVEL 9

LEVEL P

LEVEL 11

STAIRWELLS

BRIAR LABEL
BACON
SOUP

BRING HOME THE BACON

There are forty-two cans of Bacon Soup scattered throughout the studio in Chapter 3. Be sure to get them all for the "Bring Home the Bacon" Achievement.

LEVEL K

- Three cans, when you made Boris his Bacon Soup in the safehouse.
- One can, after opening the door to the safehouse, do not leave. Head back to the bathroom, where a previously locked stall on the left is now open. A can will be in the toilet.
- Four cans, three in front of the tall "Tasty Eats" crates, one between the "Tasty Eats" containers, obscured by cobwebs.
- One can, in the bottom of a shelving unit on your left.
- Two cans, on the floor around the corner from the previous shelf.
- One can, on a shelf at eye level, on your left.
- Two cans, on a desk to your right.

LEVEL 9

- One can, on the floor near a crate.
- One can, on the floor beside a pile of crates, obscured by a cobweb.

LEVEL 11

- Two cans, one on the crate in front of the door, another on the table.

LEVEL P

- One can, on the shelf beside the elevator.
- Four cans, one on a desk to the left of the doorway as you walk in, two on the crate to the left of the final valve puzzle, one on the floor beside the crate.

STAIRWELLS

- Eleven cans, in the stairwell above Level P, seven on a shelf loaded with bowls, four on a table beside a Little Miracle Station.
- One can, stairwell above Level 11, the desk on your left.
- Six cans, two stairwells above Level 11, on the floor to the right of a toilet.
- One can, stairwell below Level K, on top of a dresser, beside the ink cans.

HEARING VOICES

You'll need to listen to all the audio logs in this chapter for the "Hearing Voices" achievement:

- Shawn Flynn, Level K, alcove in the Heavenly Toys workshop
- Joey Drew, Level K, take the path of the Demon
- Susie Campbell, Level K, take the path of the Angel
- Wally Franks and Thomas Connor, Level K, before you hit the Butcher Gang poster, turn right into a new corridor
- Thomas Connor, Level 9, get off the elevator and go straight, descending the stairs toward Alice's domain
- Susie Campbell, Level 9, as you walk across the boards of the ink-flooded room, an audio log appears in the back right corner of the room
- Wally Franks, Level 11, just outside the room with the window
- Grant Cohen, Level 9, inside the boarded-up office
- Norman Polk, Level 14, on a crate just outside the Projectionist's domain
- Henry Stein, Level P, sunken room (see page 69)

Henry Stein, Level P, sunken room (see page 69)

New Objective:
COLLECT FIVE INK HEARTS

Take the elevator down to Level 14, where you'll encounter the Projectionist. You can avoid the Projectionist by staying out of his light while you gather the Ink Hearts. You can also choose to fight him, a difficult task, but one that will make gathering the hearts faster.

WEAPON	NUMBER OF HITS TO DEFEAT
GENT PIPE	72
TOMMY GUN	16
AXE	8

You can find the Ink Hearts in the following locations:

- The first Ink Heart appears in the hands of a dead Striker as you head out of the elevator.

- Take a left as you enter the Projectionist's domain. A second Ink Heart can be found in the hands of a dead Piper, across from a Little Miracle Station.

- Follow the path and continue straight to find a third Ink Heart near a dead Fisher.

- Continue on the path to find another Ink Heart on your right, near another dead Striker.

- Take a right at the forking path and continue straight until you hit a wall, and another dead Fisher, with the final Ink Heart.

Voice of
NORMAN POLK

Now I'm not lookin' for trouble. It's just the nature of us Projectionists to seek out the dark places.

You see, I've learned the ins and outs of this here studio. I know how to avoid being bothered by the likes of this . . . company.

That projectionist, they always say, creeping around, he's just lookin' for trouble. Well trouble or not, I see everything. They don't even know when I'm watchin'.

Even when I'm right behind 'em.

New Objective:
RETURN TO THE ANGEL

HENRY'S SECRET AUDIO LOG

After collecting all the Ink Hearts, exit the Projectionist's domain and head to the left of the stairs. You'll see an area that's been boarded off. Break through two sets of doors with the axe or Gent pipe to access a secret valve. Turn the valve to drain a secret corridor within the stairwell on Level P. Enter the Level P stairwell corridor (descending a flight of stairs) to hear a secret audio log from Henry.

Voice of
HENRY

Only two weeks into this company and already it's gotten interesting. Joey is a man of ideas . . . And only ideas.

When I agreed to start this whole thing with him, I thought there would be a little more give and take. Instead I give, and he takes. I haven't seen Linda for days now.

Still, someone has to make this happen. When in doubt, just keep drawing, Henry.

On the plus side, I've got a new character I think people are going to love.

New Objective:
RETURN TO THE SURFACE

Once you're finished with everything you wanted to do, return to Alice on Level 9, placing the Ink Hearts in the drop box. Alice will instruct you to return to the lift for your reward.

Upon entering the lift, Alice will accuse you of stealing from her—revealing that she wants to sacrifice Boris to help make her beautiful again. Alice will quickly take the reins back on the elevator, plunging both you and Boris down below, where you will crash.

After coming to, you'll see Boris panicking, and Alice Angel walking behind him, before he is dragged away from you.

CHAPTER FOUR
"COLOSSAL WONDERS"

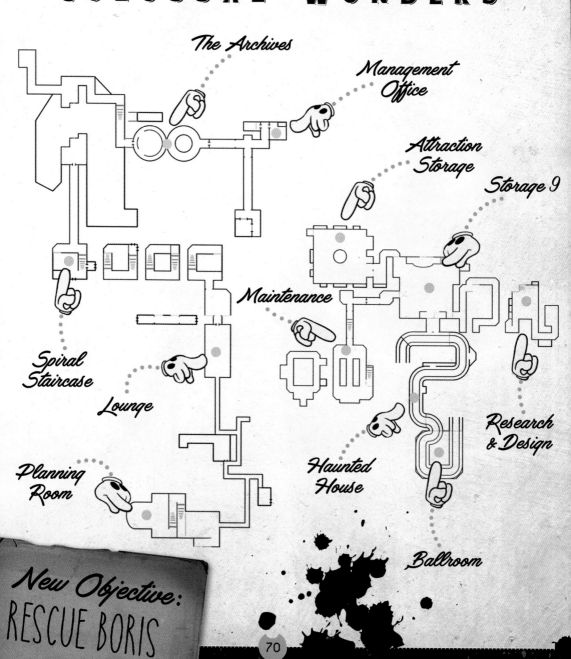

The Archives

Management Office

Attraction Storage

Storage 9

Maintenance

Spiral Staircase

Lounge

Research & Design

Planning Room

Haunted House

Ballroom

New Objective:
RESCUE BORIS

Accounting & Finance

As our Accounting & Finance Department is always reminding us, "Time is money," so we'll make this brief! Accounting & Finance handles the flow of money within our company, from the largest investments to the revenue generated by a single theater ticket. Unfortunately, all the dreaming we do here at Joey Drew Studios comes at a cost. New projects like Bendyland or the launching of a new character require a sizeable initial investment, which our accounting office balances against potential returns on that investment. That's a fancy way of saying that we have to spend money to make money.

Aside from managing revenue and investments, Accounting & Finance also handles many matters that directly affect your day to day. With mediation from the Administration Department, Accounting has final approval over department budgets, salaries, new hires, etc. Should you encounter any issues with your paycheck, your claim will likely go through Accounting with the help of Administration.

Whatever your concerns may be, if it's a money matter, it's likely under the jurisdiction of the dedicated staff of Accounting & Finance!

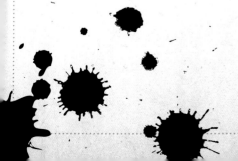

From: Grant Cohen, Accounting & Finance

RE: Employee Backpay

Valued Employee,

You are receiving this letter to notify you that you are owed BACKPAY
IN THE AMOUNT OF $60.76. As our company awaits an influx of revenue
from recent investments, we are unable to pay you. Rest assured that we
are monitoring the situation closely and will offer you relief as soon
as funds become available. We do not anticipate this period to last
more than several weeks. Please feel free to visit Accounting & Finance
on Level S with any further questions.

MacArthur Steel Co.

23 Baker Street, Brooklyn, NY
Telephone 5-4855

Quality Steel since 1874

Date June 23, 1944
Sold to Bertrum Piedmont, Joey Drew Studios

# Units	Item	Price	Amount
			$4,928.56
104	Industrial-Grade Steel	$47.39	$4,928.56
Total Debits			$0
Total Credits			$4,928.56
Net Sale			

Ticket No. 204-632

PAST DUE - 180 DAYS

PLEASE REMIT PAYMENT IMMEDIATELY

Receipts and Disbursements

July 1, 1944 to August 1, 1944
Receipts:

Investor Deposit, J. Dempsey	$24,800.00
Royalties, Heavenly Toys	$43,142.43
Box Office Sales	$56,879.18
Total Receipts	$124,821.61

Disbursements:

Employee Salaries	
Restocking Supplies	$56,659.74
Distribution Fees	$18,982.50
Marketing/Publicity	$9,842.31
Special Projects	$10,372.12
Taxes & Fees	
Total Disbursements	$64,921.98
Cash in Bank	$24,964.32
Balance as of August 2, 1944	$185,742.97
	$61,738.65
	$817.29

*Mister Drew, we can't afford these high figures on special projects any longer.
Please limit your spending or find additional investors — we're on the verge of
being in the red again this year.*

BEFORE YOU GO...
After opening the door to the Archives, the door across from the Management Office will be unlocked. This room contains both a can of Bacon Soup and theMeatly!

JOEY DR

New Objective:
ENTER THE ARCHIVES
LEVEL **S**
ACCOUNTING & FINANCE

MANAGEMENT OFFICE
◀ GRANT COHEN ▶

◀ ARCHIVES J-L

◀ R&D ACCESS

After waking up from the elevator crash, walk straight down the corridor until you reach the directory. The Archives are accessible via a door to the left, but the door is missing its valve. You'll need to find it.

Turn around and continue down the corridor toward the Accounting & Finance Management Office. The door on your left will be locked, but Grant Cohen's office, on the right, is open. Inside you'll find the door valve on the ground near a pipe on the far left wall. You may listen to the audio log here, but it'll be indiscernible. Return the valve to the door and enter the Archives.

From: Grant Cohen

To: Joey Drew

Mister Drew, I really do need to speak with you as soon as possible. Like I said in my last note, we're running $48,128 short this quarter. We won't be able to cover our taxes; I'm fielding daily calls from the IRS looking for our payments. There's not enough in the accounts right now to cover everything, even if I move some funds around and fudge the numbers. I've also received several sizeable bills from Gent, which I'll need to account for, besides the Bendyland payments, which we won't be able to make again this month. Can you please have your girl call down to me when you're next available?

Voice of
UNKNOWN

(Indiscernible)

Voice of
SUSIE CAMPBELL

They told me I was perfect for the role. Absolutely perfect.

Now Joey's going around saying things behind closed doors.

I can always tell.

Now he wants to meet again tomorrow, says he has an "opportunity" for me.

I'll hear him out. But if that smooth talker thinks he can double-cross an angel and get away with it, well, oh he's got another thing coming.

Alice, ooh, she doesn't like liars.

Directions:

Entering into the Archives, you'll see several inky figures clustered around a Bendy statue. These inky figures are called the Lost Ones. Once the music finishes playing, you'll get a new objective.

New Objective:
LOCATE THE SECRET PASSAGE

To locate the Secret Passage, head to the back of the next circular room. Push in the glowing book beside the door labeled "Private," and one of the lights above the door will turn on. You can keep track of how many books you've found by looking at the lightbulbs. When all the lightbulbs are on, you will be able to enter the Secret Passage. Push in four more books that are sticking out on the shelves: Two of them are located on the outer wall of the library room, and two are located on the inner wall. After pushing in the first three books, the screen will glitch for a moment, and the Lost Ones in the previous room will disappear.

New Objective:
ENTER THE DARKNESS

Through the Secret Passage you'll enter a dark cavern with a bridge. Interact with the lever to find that the bridge is missing a gear; you'll need to make a new gear to fix it.

New Objective:
REPAIR THE BRIDGE

Continue inside, to the safe-lined corridor. In the room at the end of the hall, pull the switch on your left to expose a well of ink. Turn the valve to summon a Swollen Searcher. Once the Searcher appears in the well, you'll be able to grab some of its thick ink and take it to the Ink Maker machine in the next room. Make sure the Ink Maker's dial on the right side of the machine is pointed to the gear that you want, then activate it and take the gear you've created to the bridge. This will grant you access to a bridge cart that will take you to the other side.

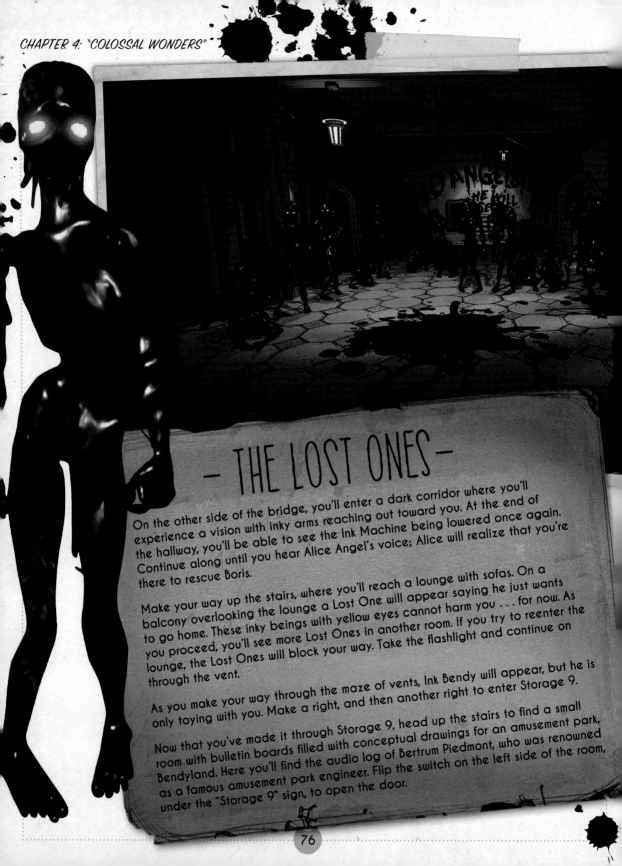

— THE LOST ONES —

On the other side of the bridge, you'll enter a dark corridor where you'll experience a vision with inky arms reaching out toward you. At the end of the hallway, you'll be able to see the Ink Machine being lowered once again. Continue along until you hear Alice Angel's voice; Alice will realize that you're there to rescue Boris.

Make your way up the stairs, where you'll reach a lounge with sofas. On a balcony overlooking the lounge a Lost One will appear saying he just wants to go home. These inky beings with yellow eyes cannot harm you . . . for now. As you proceed, you'll see more Lost Ones in another room. If you try to reenter the lounge, the Lost Ones will block your way. Take the flashlight and continue on through the vent.

As you make your way through the maze of vents, Ink Bendy will appear, but he is only toying with you. Make a right, and then another right to enter Storage 9.

Now that you've made it through Storage 9, head up the stairs to find a small room with bulletin boards filled with conceptual drawings for an amusement park, Bendyland. Here you'll find the audio log of Bertrum Piedmont, who was renowned as a famous amusement park engineer. Flip the switch on the left side of the room, under the "Storage 9" sign, to open the door.

NO ANGELS! HE WILL SET US FREE!

Voice of
BERTRUM PIEDMONT

For forty years, I've built attractions that stagger the imagination! Colossal wonders such as the world has never seen! I have earned my legacy with sweat.

But right in front of everyone... high level investors, Wall Street tycoons, the ever-tactless Joey Drew introduces me, the great Bertrum Piedmont, as Bertie! Like I was his child.

You may be paying me, Mister Drew! But you don't own me! I'll build you a park bigger than anything YOU could ever possibly conceive! But before you go taking any bows, Mister Drew, know that this grand achievement will belong to me ... and to me alone.

JOEY DREW STUDIOS ANNOUNCES BENDYLAND

New York, NY—The world-renowned animators at Joey Drew Studios have been dreaming of their own amusement park for more than a decade now, and it seems those dreams are about to come true. Joey Drew Studios has just announced its newest endeavor: Bendyland. The massive amusement park, centered around the iconic Bendy and the studio's other animated creations, is slated to open sometime next year.

"Our mission is to bring dreams to everyday life," said Joey Drew, founder and president of the company. "We can think of no more perfect way to do that than to build an amusement park designed for people of all ages. At Bendyland, imagination comes to life—literally."

Mister Drew wouldn't tell us more about when the groundbreaking will begin or where the amusement park will be

located, but public records have indicated several large tracts of the Meadowlands in southern New Jersey have been bought up by Drew's company.

Mister Drew was, however, quite forthcoming about the many attractions his park will feature. Bendyland will include motion rides, themed food and drink, and costumed characters. But aside from the basic midway fare, Drew insists there will be some major innovative surprises for fans of his films.

"For us, making Bendy real is important. The most important," continued Drew. "I was thrilled to hire Bertrum Piedmont for this task, or Bertie, as I like to call him. The amusement park is going swimmingly and I can't wait to unveil some of the colossal wonders we have in store for our fans."

Stay tuned for further updates on this exciting development.

Level S, Storage 9

If you have managed to gain employment at our studio, you likely already know about our exciting new endeavor: Bendyland! This amusement park for fans of all ages is sure to bring droves of families to our incredible cartoons, but right now, it's still in its early development.

To that end, Storage 9 and its adjacent Research & Design area on Level S are off-limits to all employees who are not stationed there for their daily work. This site contains active construction on several attractions, as well as cutting-edge technology that is considered unsafe for untrained hands. Please be sure to stay out of this area to avoid getting hurt.

Employees working in the warehouse are encouraged to wear the protective gear provided for them. Conditions in Storage 9 will likely change day to day as construction on Bendyland ramps up, so please remain alert and prepared to take on the tasks given to you. While it may be tempting, we ask our warehouse employees to refrain from playing games or interacting with unfinished rides due to safety concerns.

Regardless of your role in our company, we are excited to share more information about Bendyland as it develops. We may even have you, our valued employees, test out some of the attractions and games once they're ready for human contact! Until then, please stay safe.

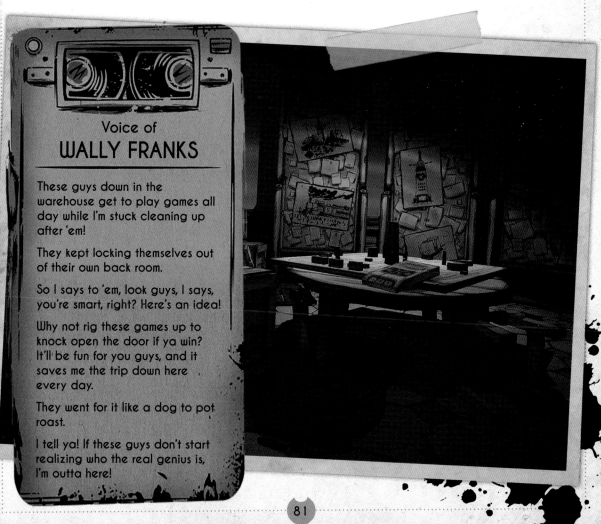

Voice of
WALLY FRANKS

These guys down in the warehouse get to play games all day while I'm stuck cleaning up after 'em!

They kept locking themselves out of their own back room.

So I says to 'em, look guys, I says, you're smart, right? Here's an idea!

Why not rig these games up to knock open the door if ya win? It'll be fun for you guys, and it saves me the trip down here every day.

They went for it like a dog to pot roast.

I tell ya! If these guys don't start realizing who the real genius is, I'm outta here!

New Objective:
POWER THE HAUNTED HOUSE

You'll enter a new room, a giant warehouse where all the Bendyland games, attractions, rides, etc., are stored. Head to the power station at the front of the room to get your new objective: Find four switches that power the Haunted House. You can follow the cords at the power station to find each switch.

To access the switches, you'll need to enter additional rooms, but the rooms are locked. You can access the first switch by winning the Bendyland mini-games. Once you win each mini-game, a sound cue will play (you don't need a perfect score), and a door will open at the foot of the stairs where you entered the warehouse.

Inside are three creepy Bendy mascot costumes, and the first switch.

Bendyland Mini-Games

Mister Drew, here are the game concepts for the midway, as requested. These will bring in quite a nice amount of revenue for the park.

BOTTLE

STRENGTH TESTER

Classic strongman game. Pick up the mallet and hit the target to try to ring the bell. Your hit will be scored: "Weak!," "Man Baby!," "Brute!," and "Super!" This game has nothing to do with strength. It's all about timing.

BOTTLE WALLOP

Classic knock 'em down game. Take the three balls on the counter and toss them at three stacks of three bottles. Knock over all nine of the bottles in order to win the game. We'll make a killing here—players don't know that the bottles are specially weighted. They're best off aiming at the lower necks of the two bottom bottles.

BULL'S-EYE BONANZA

Use the toy gun to hit different targets as they appear; do not hit the targets with an "X" through them. Destroy all good targets in order to win. The speed of this will make it particularly difficult, plus the gun will only be loaded with enough bullets for the correct number of targets. Miss a shot, and you've already lost.

—RESEARCH & DESIGN—

Head back to the power station and flip the first switch. It will open the door to your left, to Research & Design. Here you'll find the Butcher Gang, standing around a burning barrel below. You must throw the empty Bacon Soup cans to lure them away to another part of the room while you slip by. Note that these enemies cannot be defeated with the empty cans until after you throw the second switch and open the door to leave the area.

You'll find the second power switch by taking a left at the burning barrel. Back here you'll find another Lost One in a caged-off room. Continue back into the workshop, where there is a half-finished, animatronic Bendy, and an audio log from Lacie Benton.

Voice of LACIE BENTON

The only thing that works around here is my ulcer. Half these people don't know a wrench from a dang steamroller. Buncha morons is what they are. Spend their day in the warehouse arguin' over who's supposed to be doin' what or playing them silly games. Still, I'm not complainin'. I get most of my time to myself. Suits me just fine. Only thing that bothers me is that mechanical demon in the corner. Bertrum's been working on it for a month now. Says it will walk someday and maybe dance. All it does now is give me the creeps. I swear, when my back's turned . . . that thing's movin'.

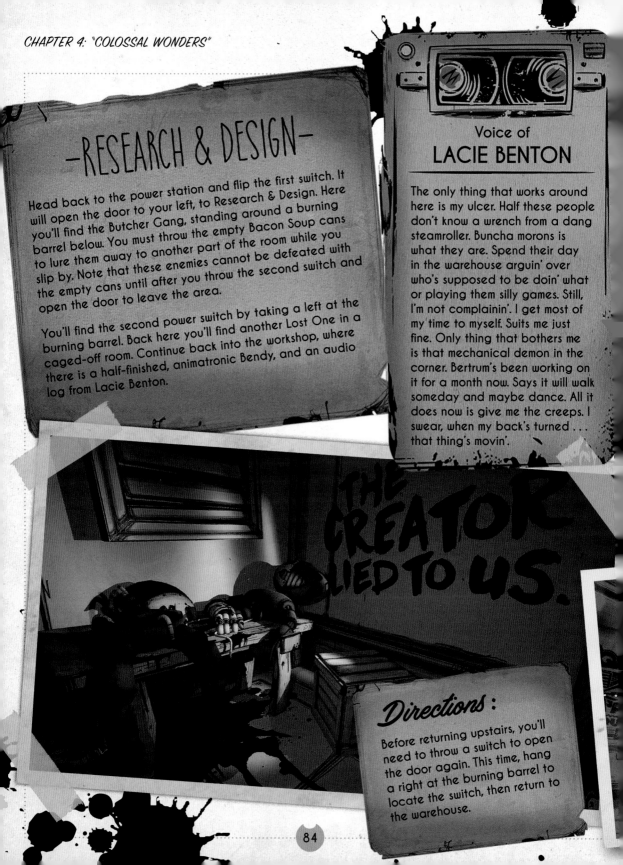

THE CREATOR LIED TO US.

Directions:

Before returning upstairs, you'll need to throw a switch to open the door again. This time, hang a right at the burning barrel to locate the switch, then return to the warehouse.

Directions:

Throw the second switch at the power station to open the door to "Attraction Storage."

After winding your way along the corridor, you'll come to a big open room with a ride in the center. Play the audio log on the table and get ready for a fight.

Directions:

Once the audio log is over, Bertrum will smash the desk in front of you. In the shards of the desk you'll find an axe. Wield the axe against the glowing joints on the arms of the ride. Bertrum will throw his arms around, smashing one against the ground until it goes limp. That is your chance to move in and hack off the joint screws (four per arm). Once all four joint screws are off, the arm will break. Hack off the four joint screws on all four limbs to defeat Bertrum. Once he's defeated you will lose your axe, but you will be able to unlock the third power switch.

LIFT
CONTROL

MAINTENANCE

Throw the third switch at the power station to open the door to Maintenance. As you descend the stairs, beware; the Projectionist is lurking about. Pull the lever for the "Lift Control" on the right side of the room. The Projectionist will scream and try to chase you, so head upstairs to the balcony that wraps around the room. Here there is another lever for the power, which you'll need to pull. Once you do, the Projectionist will appear to vanish. Head down the stairs, to the left side of the room, where you'll find an audio log from Joey Drew.

Directions:

Continue back up the steps toward the exit, but the exit is locked. The Projectionist will pursue you, so hide in the Little Miracle Station, where you will watch Bendy destroy the Projectionist right in front of you. When the scene is over, you'll be able to exit and activate the final switch at the power station in the warehouse.

Voice of
JOEY DREW

I believe there's something special in all of us. With true inner strength, you can conquer even your biggest challenges. You just have to believe in yourself and remain honest, motivated, and above all, who you really are.

Okay, let's stop it right there. I can only do so many takes of this trash a day. And tell the guys in writing I want more use of the word *dreaming* in every message. Keep railing on that, get it? Dreaming! Dreaming! Dreaming! People just eat up that kind of slop. Hmm. What? It's still on? Well, turn it off, damn it!

OVERACHIEVER!

A few achievements will be given to you through the natural course of the story:

AROUND AND AROUND: Defeat Bertrum Piedmont.

HAUNTING WE WILL GO: Restore power to the Haunted House.

REUNITED: Find Boris.

But before you head inside the Haunted House to finish *Chapter 4: "Colossal Wonders,"* be sure to check the following items off your to-do list:

BARBECUED: Visit theMeatly. (You can find him in the room opposite Grant Cohen's office. Walk through the "Sheep Songs" poster on the wall. Unlike other chapters, where you cannot access him until near the end of the chapter, you can visit theMeatly as soon as you unlock the Archives door.)

FINGER WAGGIN': Turn on the radio in Chapter 4. (In the caverns outside the Archives, use the Ink Maker machine to create a radio. Turn it on to gain this achievement.)

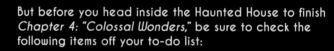

WASTING TIME: Ring the bell. (Get a "Super!" on the Strength Tester mini-game.)

BULL'S-EYE: Get a perfect score on the Bull's-Eye Bonanza mini-game.

CALL THE MILK MAN: Get a perfect score on the Bottle Wallop mini-game.

GOING TO BE SICK: Go for a wild ride. (While fighting Bertrum, wait until he lays his arm down, then try to interact with the cart. Doing so will allow you to ride without dying. Don't get sick!)

A LITTLE SOUVENIR: Take a photo at the photo cutout. (In the Maintenance room, climb the stairs to the walkway above the inky floor. There you'll find a cardboard cutout of a figure with a trident. Walk behind it and look through the hole at the camera, which will snap a photo.)

STILL LISTENING: Listen to all the audio logs in Chapter 4 (see page 92).

JUST LIKE MOM USED TO MAKE: Collect all the Bacon Soup in Chapter 4 (see page 91).

UNLIKELY VICTORY: Complete Chapter 4 with the plunger (see page 93).

STUDIO LAYOUT

BRIAR LABEL
BACON SOUP

JUST LIKE MOM USED TO MAKE

There are nineteen cans of Bacon Soup scattered throughout the studio in Chapter 4. Be sure to get them all for the "Just Like Mom Used to Make" achievement.

- One can, on the floor to your right outside the elevator.

- One can, in the trash bin. (This door will unlock after you open the Archives door.)

- One can, on the floor behind a TV, beside a desk.

- One can, to the left of the inky well where the Swollen Searcher appears.

- One can, at eye level on a shelf to your right as you ascend the stairs.

- One can, inside the trunk to the left of the doorway.

- One can, on the floor between a crate and a bulletin board.

- One can, on the ledge of an empty games booth, to the right of the Bottle Wallop.

- Two cans, one on the railing to the right of the door as you enter, another on the barrel near the first can, surrounded by empty cans.

- One can, lying on its side on top of the first shelving unit as you enter the animatronic workshop.

- Two cans, one to the right of a dead Striker, another opposite the Striker, on top of a crate.

- Two cans, one to the left as you walk in, hidden behind a barrel, another to the left of the giant mouth, on a crate.

- One can, under the "Buddy Boris Railway" poster, under one of the pistons.

- One can, on top of a barrel in the corner, on the balcony.

- One can, as you enter the Haunted House, search under the seat of one of the empty carts to your right.

- One can, on the table, to the left of the pipe organ.

—STILL LISTENING—

You'll need to listen to all the audio logs in this chapter for the "Still Listening" achievement:

- Unknown, Grant Cohen's office
- Susie Campbell, second Archives room
- Bertrum Piedmont, Bendyland concept room, before Bendyland warehouse
- Wally Franks, Bendyland warehouse, between Bottle Wallop and Bull's-Eye Bonanza
- Lacie Benton, Research & Design, animatronic room
- Bertrum Piedmont, Attractions, Bertrum's room
- Joey Drew, Maintenance, Projectionist's lair

—ARM YOURSELF!—

- **GENT PIPE:** If you don't take any of the below steps, you will face the final boss with the Gent pipe.

- **PLUNGER:** After you pull the fourth lever to access the Haunted House, return to Maintenance. Descend the stairs to the inky abyss, then head upstairs to the balcony area. To the left of the power lever is a chest; open it and retrieve the dial inside. During the final battle of Chapter 4, interact with the Ink Maker, which will have a new setting to make the plunger.

- **EMPTY BACON SOUP CANS:** After you pull the second lever for the Haunted House, return to the Research & Design animatronic room, where you can stock up on as many as thirty-one empty Bacon Soup cans in the shelves across from the Bendy animatronic. You can take these out of the room and use them to defeat the final boss (or any other enemy in Chapter 4) without the hassle of the Ink Maker. Defeating the final boss in this way will trigger a flashing hallucination.

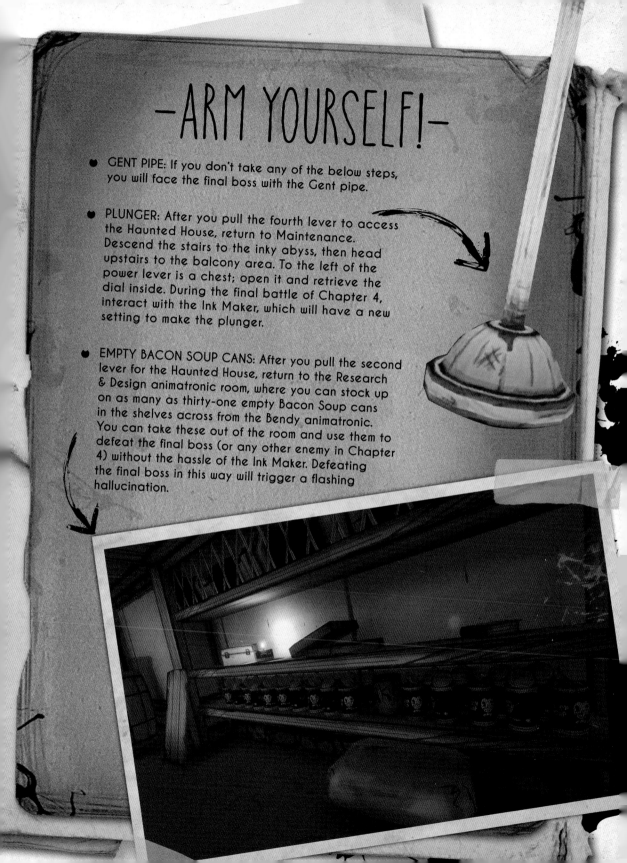

New Objective: DEFEAT BORIS

—INSIDE THE HAUNTED HOUSE—

With all switches activated, the Haunted House opens! You will need to get into a roller-coaster cart in order to proceed, despite passing a "Turn Back" sign.

After boarding, you'll hear Alice Angel's voice, taunting you for wanting to rescue Boris. When she's done speaking, you'll enter a massive, dimly lit room with sofas, barrels, and a warmly lit chandelier. Here you'll be reunited with Boris, but Alice has modified him a bit. It is now your task to defeat this "new and improved" Brute Boris.

—BRINGING DOWN BRUTE BORIS—

1. Dodge Brute Boris's attacks as he runs into the walls, trying to attack you. Beware: Two hits from him will land you at the respawn point.

2. He'll start bleeding ink for a few seconds. Stop and collect the thick ink that Brute Boris leaves behind.

3. Use the Ink Maker and the thick ink to create the Gent pipe or plunger if you retrieved the special gear.

4. When Brute Boris runs into another wall and bleeds again, hit him with your weapon. Any weapons made with the Ink Maker are good for one use only, so your weapon will break after a strike.

5. Brute Boris will now start jumping about the room, trying to smash you. Again, two hits will bring you down.

6. Wait until Brute Boris starts bleeding ink again, collect it, and put it into the Ink Maker to create a new weapon. Hit him while he is bleeding. Your weapon will disappear again.

7. Brute Boris will now pick up roller-coaster carts as they enter the room and try to throw them at you. If one cart hits you, you will die.

8. Dodge the carts, wait until he starts bleeding, and collect his ink. Put it into the Ink Maker to make your final weapon. One more hit will bring Brute Boris down for good.

Once the battle is over, you will encounter two new figures—a blade-wielding angel and someone who looks very much like Boris used to.

If you gave Boris a bone in Chapter 3, and played straight through to Chapter 4, Brute Boris will still have the bone in his mouth.

CHAPTER FIVE
"THE LAST REEL"

Administration

Administration Lobby

Ink River

Gent Home Office

Office of
Joey Drew

Film Vault

Giant Ink Machine

Ink Machine
Pump Station

Throne Room

Mr. & Mrs. Frederick Pendle request
the honor of your presence at the
marriage of their daughter,

Allison

to

Mr. Thomas J. Connor

on Saturday, the twenty-third day of February
nineteen hundred and fifty-two
at two-thirty in the afternoon
at First Light Presbyterian Church

Reception to follow

Joey,
You and your studio brought us together. You should
be with us on our wedding day. Hope you'll join us.
—Allison

Mister Joey Drew

X̶ Regretfully declines
——— Will attend

Directions:

As the chapter opens, you'll be introduced to two new characters: Alice and Tom. They're not sure if they can trust you, so they have you locked up in their hideout.

The screen will fade, and then you will hear Alice telling Tom that she will be gone for "only a few hours" to explore Level 6. Tom will watch over you now, wielding an axe. When you wake up, Alice will offer you some Bacon Soup, but Tom will snatch it away with an angry expression on his face.

When you next wake, Alice will tell you a few things . . .

- Everyone writes on the walls. According to Alice, "For some poor souls down here, it's the only way they can be heard."
- Don't touch the ink for too long or else it can claim you.
- Alice met Tom when he rescued her from some risky business.
- While mapping one of the floors of the studio, Alice discovered that if she looked through a certain piece of glass, she could see hidden messages. She then gives you the Seeing Tool.

— WIELDING THE SEEING TOOL —

Alice will hand you the Seeing Tool, which you can use to discover hidden messages. Move around to reveal secrets in this scene.

- "She will leave you for dead" is written on the wall behind Alice.

- A halo around Alice's head

After using the Seeing Tool, Alice will admit that she thinks she isn't meant to leave the studio, but perhaps you are— she thinks you might be "the hope I've been waiting for."

Alice will tell you to sleep and wake up tomorrow. The screen will fade, and later you'll hear Alice arguing with Tom. Tom did something rash to alert Ink Bendy of their location. A little while later, Ink Bendy has found the hideout. Although Alice will try to free you from the barricade, she won't be able to, and Alice and Tom will leave.

SHE WILL LEAVE YOU FOR DEAD

YOU DRAW BEAUTIFULLY

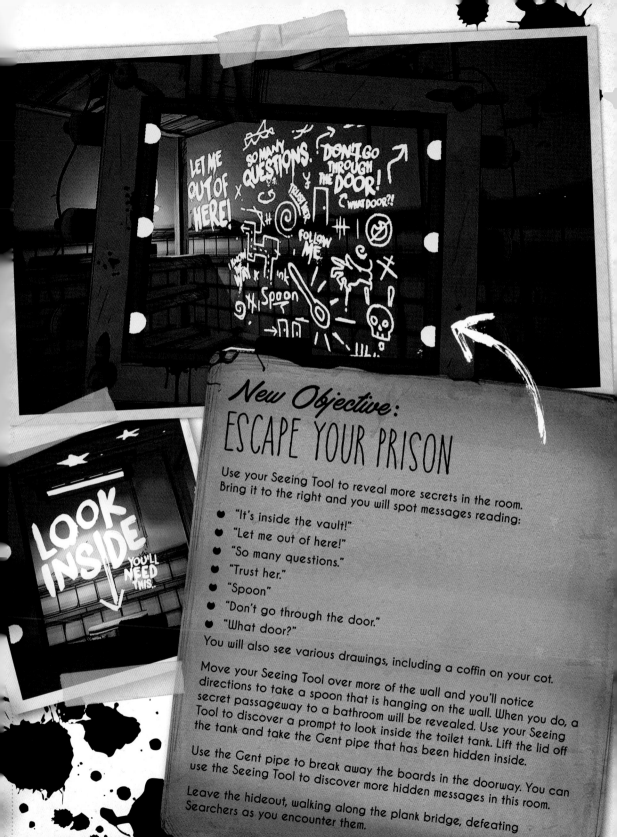

New Objective:
ESCAPE YOUR PRISON

Use your Seeing Tool to reveal more secrets in the room.
Bring it to the right and you will spot messages reading:

- "It's inside the vault!"
- "Let me out of here!"
- "So many questions."
- "Trust her."
- "Spoon"
- "Don't go through the door."
- "What door?"

You will also see various drawings, including a coffin on your cot.

Move your Seeing Tool over more of the wall and you'll notice
directions to take a spoon that is hanging on the wall. When you do, a
secret passageway to a bathroom will be revealed. Use your Seeing
Tool to discover a prompt to look inside the toilet tank. Lift the lid off
the tank and take the Gent pipe that has been hidden inside.

Use the Gent pipe to break away the boards in the doorway. You can
use the Seeing Tool to discover more hidden messages in this room.

Leave the hideout, walking along the plank bridge, defeating
Searchers as you encounter them.

New Objective:
LAUNCH THE BARGE

Using your Seeing Tool, you will discover a hidden message that reads, "There's something in the river." Pull the lever toward you to move the Ink Barge forward, and then pull it again to launch it into the Ink River. Now you'll be able to jump onto the barge.

New Objective:
FOLLOW THE INK RIVER

Navigate the Ink Barge by using its throttle. You'll descend through a tunnel to a new room, but before getting there you'll need to unclog the barge's paddle wheel periodically with your Gent pipe. After the first time it clogs, you'll see a giant Bendy hand destroy another barge. You'll need to navigate the barge away quickly to not be pulled under by the hand.

Once you've escaped, you'll be taken to a new location called the Lost Harbor.

— THE LOST HARBOR —

Use your Seeing Tool to discover a hidden message that reads, "Once people, now fallen into despair." Another hidden message says, "You bring death."

By navigating closely to the barricaded door you'll trigger Sammy Lawrence, who breaks down the barriers and comes after you with an axe. You'll need to dodge his attacks and use the Gent pipe to knock his mask off his face. Approach him again and he will throw you to the ground, after which Alice and Tom will rescue you.

After Sammy Lawrence fades away, Tom will offer you an axe. Hordes of Searchers, Miner Searchers, and Lost Ones will spawn to attack you. (For the first time, these Lost Ones are enemies and can harm you.) Destroy them all with your axe; Alice and Tom will help you.

ENEMY	NUMBER OF HITS TO DEFEAT
SEARCHER	1
LOST ONE	2
MINER SEARCHER	4

This will be a lengthy battle, but when it's over, Alice will ask you to lead the way out.

To escape the Lost Harbor, use your axe to break down the barriers on the path to the left of where Sammy Lawrence emerged.

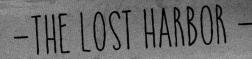

JOEY DREW STUDIOS UNDER INVESTIGATION

FINANCIAL TROUBLE LOOMING FOR ANIMATION COMPANY

New York, NY—Joey Drew Studios is under investigation, with former employees citing hazardous work environments, harassment, and excessive backpay. The company is also in danger of going bankrupt, according to investors.

"These accusations are preposterous—they're ridiculous," said Joey Drew, founder and president of the company. "I vehemently deny them. These are sad lies no doubt made by disgruntled former employees or competing studios. Our facility is state-of-the-art. Joey Drew Studios is where dreams happen. And it's where dreams are going to happen. We have no financial troubles at all."

Anonymous workers at Joey Drew Studios have threatened to unionize over the poor conditions, which include unpermitted building, hazardous electrical wiring, and a plumbing system prone to bursting. Many employees also cite excessive work hours, most of which were unpaid. Several animators confided that they hadn't seen their families in weeks, after being threatened with disciplinary action and termination if they were unable to finish animations on exceedingly tight schedules.

Music director Sammy Lawrence seemed unfazed by the claims. "Joey runs a pretty tight ship. Some people can't take it, and that's fine. This industry is all about survival of the fittest. We don't need a bunch of useless sheep who can't finish their work on time."

Despite the mounting evidence against the company, Mister Drew remains adamant that the studio has done nothing wrong.

"I am so certain that there's nothing wrong with our studio, I not only welcome

investigators—I invite them," said Drew. "Reports of barricaded offices, employees locked in work spaces, and malfunctioning machinery are just crazy. And about the money, why, we just installed new technology in partnership with the Gent Corporation! We certainly wouldn't have done that if we were going bankrupt! In fact, we're on the verge of taking our business to the next level. I can't wait to show everyone what we have in store with our new cartoons."

City officials have reported that they will be exploring these complaints against the company in the coming weeks, to determine if the claims have any merit. In the meantime, employees seem to be fleeing the studio in droves. Recent job listings have included a head of animation, several background and character artists, as well as inkers and storyboard artists. If his staffing issues are as bad as they seem, one must wonder if Mister Drew intends to draw future cartoons himself.

Voice of
JOEY DREW

A small memo to all administration offices!

Rumors have begun to fly that we simply can't tolerate any longer. The idea that the company is in some form of financial difficulty is untrue and a slanderous lie against us.

It's also been known to me that some backroom incompetents are not trusting in my leadership.

As a leader, I'm always steering the boat, guiding our destiny. Looking at the big picture. No need for you people to worry about such complicated things. Just do whatever it is you do and trust your leader . . . which is me.

 ▲ INK WELL

 ■ LITTLE MIRACLE STATION

 ✘ INK MAKER MACHINE

New Objective:
DRAIN THE PASSAGE

Next you'll be led into a new location with upbeat music playing, the Administration offices. You'll need to obtain missing pipes in order to drain the passage to the Film Vault.

To get these pipes, you'll need to:

1. Open the door to Administration. To do this, turn right at the Ink Maker machine in the corner of the lobby, then head through two doorways until you're behind the lobby desk. Pull the switch to open the door.
2. Collect thick ink, which you can find at the inky fountain outside the office of Joey Drew.
3. Return to the Ink Maker machine in the Administration lobby. Insert the thick ink into the Ink Maker.
4. Select the proper pipe icon on the Ink Maker's dial and turn the wheel. Tip: You will need a "T" pipe, a straight pipe, and a bent pipe, so make sure to turn the dial to the correct setting.
5. Head to the Film Vault entrance and insert the missing pipe into the piping system.
6. If you're pursued by the Butcher Gang, you can try to lose them in the maze of offices, head to a Little Miracle Station, or run into the pool of ink at the start of this area.

When all the pipes are restored, the Film Vault door will open.

Administration

Feeling a bit turned around? You must have wandered into the Administration offices! Like the oil in a finely tuned machine, Administration provides the grease that keeps our company running smoothly. Our talented administrative staff handle many vital functions to our company, such as:

- Keeping the company well stocked with supplies needed by various departments.

- Acting as mediator between Accounting and different departments to come to a healthy compromise on all budgetary concerns.

- Processing job postings, new hires, and keeping current employees happy and content in their role at our studio.

- Liaising with external companies such as Gent Corporation and Briar Label Co., and exploring new avenues for corporate partnership.

- Managing paperwork and developing new methods to make our staff even more productive.

If you should ever have a concern that falls under one of the above areas, feel free to swing by the Administrative offices. But be warned—it's a bit of a maze down here! You might want to call ahead and ask for directions.

TODAY'S APPOINTMENTS

PLEASE SIGN IN AT FRONT DESK ON ARRIVAL.
NO APPOINTMENT. NO ACCESS.

9:30	Dr. Hackenbush DVM
10:00	Bertrum Piedmont (rescheduled)
10:15	F. Fontaine
11:15	Health & Safety Board Agent
11:30	E. Misner - PP
11:45	Sammy Lawrence
12:00	Mr. Drew at lunch!
2:00	Thomas Connor - GENT
2:15	Charles and the Prodigies
2:45	M.M. meeting (out of office)
3:30	That Puppet Guy
5:30	Hayden - UAC
6:00	Susie Campbell

JOEY DREW STUDIOS

Voice of
WALLY FRANKS

So turns out it's my lucky day! I got to cleaning some of the offices around 2 a.m. last night. And what do you think I find on one of the chairs? A big freaking chocolate cake. Just sitting there! Practically yelling my name!

You know? I work hard! I earn my pay. Every darn dollar. But you know what this company's missing? Little, benefitting perks. And this here cake? It's a perk!

Hopefully no one finds out what I done. 'Cause if they did, I can tell what would happen. I'm outta here.

Our Friends at

GENT

Besides Briar Label Co., the company name you'll likely hear thrown around the studio most is Gent Corporation. After sponsoring the hit "Construction Corruption" Bendy and Boris cartoon, a truly magnificent partnership was born between Joey Drew Studios and the Gent Corporation. Our state-of-the-art studio is a testament to the innovative, can-do attitude of Gent and its employees. (And their low, low pricing helps too!)

From the elevators you likely ride each morning to the safes being locked up in the Archives each night; the valves and pipes that keep our plumbing flowing to the flashlights our handyman might use to find a blown fuse, Gent keeps this studio going day in and day out. In addition to everyday devices, Gent has also created several machines of the future, including the Ink Maker machines. With the crank of a handle this technology can spit out a functioning item made from high-quality, thick ink. Whether you need a pipe, a gear, a plunger, or a radio, the Ink Maker can build it for you at little to no cost to our company!

Best of all, Gent staff are always on call to help whenever a pipe bursts or the lights go out or you have a new machine in mind that can help increase your department's productivity!

Voice of
THOMAS CONNOR

Progress Report to the Gent Home Office.

Client: Joey Drew Studios.

Although we're making progress, the client's expectations keep changing. What started as a machine to simply mold life-size figures now seems to be teetering on the edge of magic more than engineering.

Although Mister Drew remains convinced they are the same thing.

The process of running the cartoon film through the machine for the figures to imprint upon themselves is going well. We've had several near successes.

One weird note, the first figure ever created was a foiled attempt in the likeness of the character called Bendy. Since that time, no other attempts of this particular figure have emerged. And the one that did, I dunno, there's just something unworldly about him.

Voice of
JOEY DREW

Listen, Tommy, I know you boys over at Gent are doing your best, but I'm paying for living attractions, not weird abominations!

Whatever that grinning thing was I saw wandering around your office, you better keep it locked up tight!

I realize it was a first attempt but imagine if the press caught sight of it! Might scare off investors!

And in response to your previous memo: If you claim your failures are because these things are soulless, then, damn it, we'll get them a soul!

After all, I own thousands of 'em!

Office of
Joey Drew

Since Bendy first sprang to life from Mister Joey Drew's pen in 1929, the founder and president of Joey Drew Studios has kept our business running full-steam to the forefront of animation. An accomplished animator, most of Mister Drew's time today is spent meeting with new investors and various department heads so he can best continue to steer the company on the right course.

Mister Drew keeps his office in Administration and makes it a priority

ATTENTION!

JOEY DREW STUDIOS IS NOT INTERESTED IN
THE AQUIRING OF NEW PROPERTIES THAT
ARE DERIVATIVES OF EXISTING CHARACTERS.

FOR BEST PITCH:

- BE EARLY FOR YOUR APPOINTMENT

- KEEP PITCH UNDER THREE MINUTES

- HAVE YOUR PITCH FEE CHECK READY

B

to remain accessible to his employees. If you'd like to make a one-on-one appointment, you can contact his secretary at any time. That said, you're more likely to run into Mister Drew around the studio, adjusting a storyboard in animation or attending a voice-over session in the recording booths. As the creator of Bendy, Boris the Wolf, and Alice Angel, Mister Drew views these characters and his employees as his family, and he always makes time for family. Mister Drew enjoys staying active and involved with the day-to-day happenings at his studio, so if you see him around, share something about your job that you're excited about. Better yet, share one of your dreams with him. It is Mister Drew's sincerely held belief that the lifeblood of innovation comes from the kind of crazy concepts that more pragmatic people might cast aside. Mister Drew loves to say that he got started with just "a pencil and a dream." The pencil was important, but the dream is what built this studio and continues to drive its success.

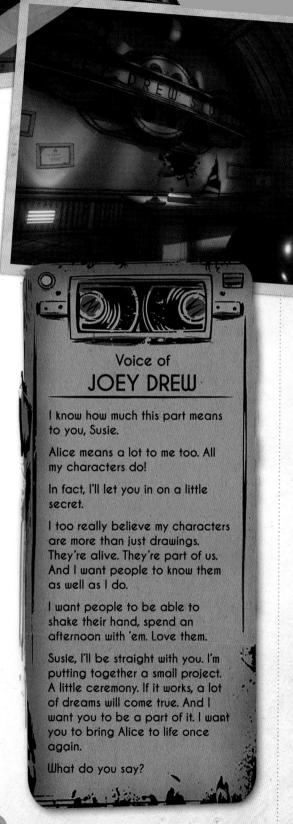

Voice of
JOEY DREW

I know how much this part means to you, Susie.

Alice means a lot to me too. All my characters do!

In fact, I'll let you in on a little secret.

I too really believe my characters are more than just drawings. They're alive. They're part of us. And I want people to know them as well as I do.

I want people to be able to shake their hand, spend an afternoon with 'em. Love them.

Susie, I'll be straight with you. I'm putting together a small project. A little ceremony. If it works, a lot of dreams will come true. And I want you to be a part of it. I want you to bring Alice to life once again.

What do you say?

Welcome to the
Film Vault!

If you're looking to watch one of the hundreds of Bendy, Boris the Wolf, or Alice Angel cartoons made right here in our studio, you've come to the right place! The Film Vault is your resource for the many hours of animated footage produced in Joey Drew Studios' fifteen-plus years of operation. Most of these films are no longer in theaters, and some have been out of circulation for years.

To schedule an appointment to review footage, simply call the office of our projectionist, Norman Polk. Mr. Polk would be pleased to assist you with reviewing whatever footage you require. You can peruse some of their fine selections on the next pages!

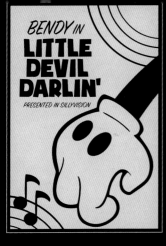

The first Bendy cartoon, "Little Devil Darlin'," helped to cement Bendy's place in the hearts of fans.

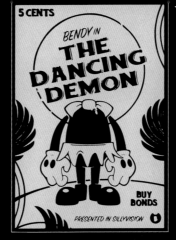

Another oldie "The Dancing Demon" was recently re-released (along with many other of our classics) in concert with the US government in an effort to raise sales on war bonds.

The first animated feature starring everyone's best buddy, Boris! Fans loved the interactions between Bendy and Boris so much that Boris became a regular cast member in Joey Drew Studios' cartoons.

This popular animated feature from the early days of the studio spawned its own line of popular toy trains from Heavenly Toys!

In 1933, the world was introduced to Alice Angel in "Sent from Above." Joey Drew Studios' own singing, dancing angel stole hearts around the country.

"Bendy and Boris Go to Hell in a Hand Basket" was our studio's first foray into longer-form animation. This cartoon featured an extended runtime as the iconic duo rides a mine cart through a dark and spooky underworld.

"Siren Serenade" was the first Alice Angel cartoon that did not feature any other Joey Drew cast members such as Bendy or Boris.

A dash of spice makes all the difference in this comedic Bendy feature from the early 1930s.

It was Bendy to the rescue in "Hellfire Fighter"!

Bendy met his first recurring villains in "The Butcher Gang"! Charley, Barley, and Edgar would never pass up an opportunity to pick on anyone—let alone a little devil like Bendy—but they get their comeuppance in the end!

Bendy was juggling more than just flaming batons in this 1937 cartoon feature.

Bendy was out for fame and glory in "Showbiz Bendy," a cartoon that saw him teaming up with Alice and Boris on a magic act on Broadway's biggest stage.

Avast ye scallywags! Bendy explored the ocean blue in "The Devil's Treasure," where he sought out a pirate's secret booty.

The Butcher Gang returned in "Demonic Tonic," in which the nefarious villains shrunk Bendy, trapping him in a bottle for their own amusement.

Bendy was on nanny duty in "Rosemary's Baby-Sitter."

Just in time for the nation's Halloween festivities, "Tombstone Picnic" debuted to send a shiver down America's spine. Bendy even came face to face with

This wintertime mini-short became a holiday classic for families around the country. Poor Bendy tries to make the perfect snowman.

Following up on the earlier success of "Tombstone Picnic," "Haunted Hijinx" saw Bendy and Boris reunited for more frightening fare!

JOEY DREW STUDIOS TIMELINE

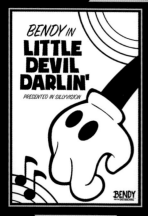

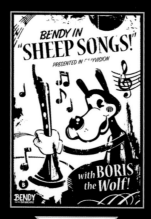

1929

Joey Drew Studios established by Joey Drew! Bendy premiered in his first cartoon, "Little Devil Darlin'," to the delight of children, many of whom had never seen a cartoon with sound before!

1929

Boris the Wolf premieres in "Sheep Songs!" The musical cartoon is an instant hit with fans, securing Boris a permanent spot in the Joey Drew family.

1933

Little girls around the country gain their own heroine when Alice Angel premieres in "Sent from Above"!

1934

Bendy is a household name! He and Boris get their own plush toys just in time for the holidays. Lines to buy these "Heavenly Toys" stretch outside the stores on Thirty-Fourth Street in New York City.

1935

Bendy finds himself in a bit of trouble when "The Butcher Gang" lands in theaters! These dastardly villains are always causing trouble for the little devil, but he finds a way to get back at them in the end.

1940

Joey Drew begins discussions with famed amusement-park designer Bertrum Piedmont on Bendyland, a state-of-the-art cartoon experience for families.

New Objective:
SEARCH THE VAULT

Once inside the vault, you'll be able to search around. Interact with the glowing box to reveal a set of tangled film reels inside. Then you'll be reunited with Alice and Tom, who used a rope to get down to the Film Vault.

Here, you reveal that Ink Bendy has something you need. You'll have to enter the Demon's lair to get it. While Alice lists off the things you'll need to find to break through the door to your right, Tom will punch the door open with brute force. You'll enter a new corridor that will seem familiar . . . You'll come upon a Bendy cutout, and nearby it is a solitary desk: yours.

Then you'll turn the corner (ignoring the painted ink that reads "Death" with an arrow pointing that way) and come upon the sprawling Ink Machine Room. Alice tells you that she and Tom can't wade their way through the ink river because they'll disappear . . . but you can.

Bought of

OVERACHIEVER!

A few achievements will be given to you through the natural course of the story:

 PIPES AND PROBLEMS: Create and place all the missing pipes to drain the passage to the Film Vault.

 SHADOWS AND SUFFERING: Discover what's living below. (Finish fighting the Searchers and Lost Ones in the Lost Harbor.)

 TO HELL AND BACK: Complete the main story.

But before you wade into the Ink Machine to finish *Chapter 5: "The Last Reel,"* be sure to check the following items off your to-do list:

 GOLDBRICKING: Let others do the work. (When you're set upon by Searchers, don't help Alice and Tom kill them for a while.)

 VALUED EMPLOYEE: Take a longer walk. (While collecting pipe segments in Administration, avoid being seen by the Butcher Gang.)

 AGGRESSION: Bathe in violence. (Don't die during the battle in the Lost Harbor.)

NO NEED FOR A SPOON: Collect all the Bacon Soup in Chapter 5 (see page 120).

 TOE TAPPIN': Turn on the radio in Chapter 5. (When you enter the second room in the Film Vault, open the box on the floor directly to your left. The radio is inside it.)

 NOW HEAR THIS!: Listen to all audio logs in Chapter 5 (see page 121).

 STANDING PROUD: Find out where you belong. (After completing the game, a new Archives chapter will unlock. In the chapter, there is a pedestal and Henry Stein's biography on a sign next to it. Jump onto the pedestal to earn this achievement.)

 A SWEET DISCOVERY: Say hello to an old friend. (After finishing the pipe puzzle, return to the Administration offices. As you approach the office of Joey Drew, turn down the hall to your left. The first door on the right opens onto an office containing a "Sheep Songs" poster. Walk through that wall to visit theMeatly.)

ULTIMATE OVERACHIEVER

If you've been keeping up with your achievements for each chapter thus far, you'll also earn the following:

 THE VOICE COLLECTOR: Listen to all audio logs in the game.

 GOLD RECORD: Turn on all of the hidden radios in the game.

 MASTER OF BACON: Collect all of the Bacon Soup in the game.

 GRAND PUPPETEER: Find theMeatly in all chapters.

STUDIO LAYOUT

NO NEED FOR A SPOON

There are seven cans of Bacon Soup scattered throughout the studio in Chapter 5. Be sure to get them all for the "No Need for a Spoon" achievement.

- Four cans, in the hideout, three on the shelf to the left as you break out of your prison; one can around the corner on your left, under a cot against the wall.

- One can, in Administration, on a chair to the right of the office of Joey Drew.

- Two cans, in Administration, on a shelf in the closet across from the office of Joey Drew.

BRIAR LABEL
BACON SOUP

NOW HEAR THIS!

You'll need to listen to all the audio logs in this chapter for the "Still Listening" achievement:

- Thomas Connor, Administration lobby; head through the doors to the pipe puzzle, then turn right into the office alcove.
- Joey Drew, Administration offices; enter Administration and enter the door at the end of the first hallway.
- Wally Franks, Administration offices; enter Administration and turn right at the end of the first hallway. Enter the office on your right.
- Joey Drew, Administration offices; enter Administration and turn right at the end of the hallway. Round the left corner and enter the office on your right. Turning left, you'll find this audio log on a table between two locked doors, under a "Gent" sign.
- Joey Drew, Administration offices; enter the office of Joey Drew.

THE SCYTHE

An incredibly powerful weapon is accessible in Chapter 5, provided you've played through the game up to this point having accomplished the following:

- Start the game from Chapter 1 and make it to the Administration offices in Chapter 5 without dying.
- In Chapter 2, crush the Miner Searcher where you crushed Swollen Jack (see page 33).
- In Chapter 3, defeat the Searcher Boss in the Lever Challenge (see page 63).
- In Chapter 4, defeat the Butcher Gang, Bertrum Piedmont, the Projectionist, and Brute Boris with the thirty-one empty Bacon Soup cans you found in Research & Design (see page 93).
- Solve the pipe puzzle to drain the Film Vault entrance and open the door, but do not head inside yet.
- Return to the Administration offices and locate a large open room in which the far wall has been removed. In the rubble, you'll find the Scythe.

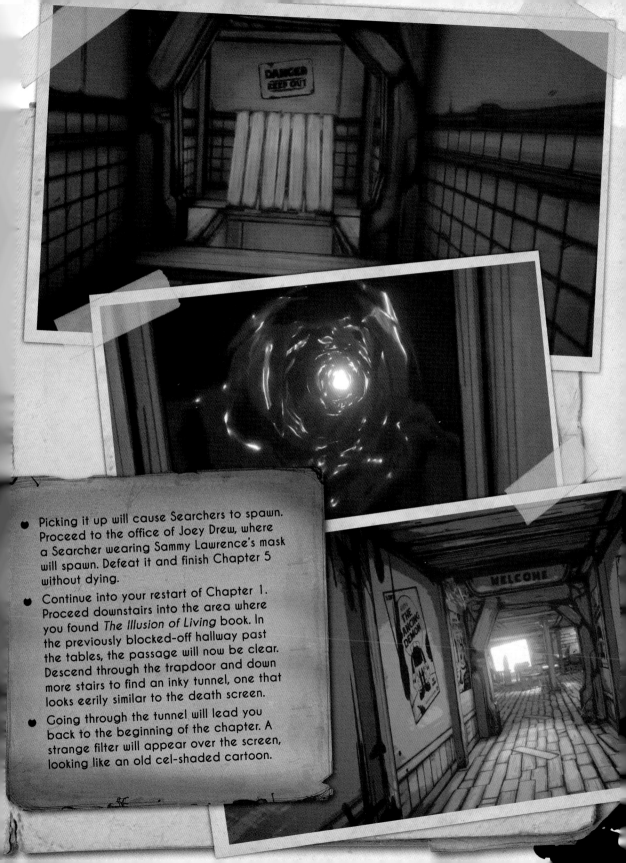

- Picking it up will cause Searchers to spawn. Proceed to the office of Joey Drew, where a Searcher wearing Sammy Lawrence's mask will spawn. Defeat it and finish Chapter 5 without dying.
- Continue into your restart of Chapter 1. Proceed downstairs into the area where you found *The Illusion of Living* book. In the previously blocked-off hallway past the tables, the passage will now be clear. Descend through the trapdoor and down more stairs to find an inky tunnel, one that looks eerily similar to the death screen.
- Going through the tunnel will lead you back to the beginning of the chapter. A strange filter will appear over the screen, looking like an old cel-shaded cartoon.

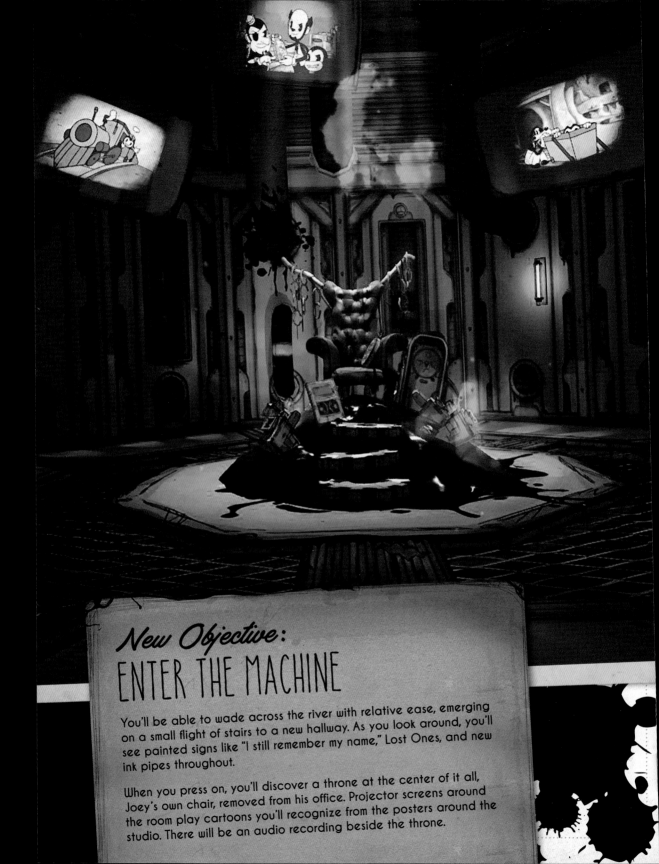

New Objective:
ENTER THE MACHINE

You'll be able to wade across the river with relative ease, emerging on a small flight of stairs to a new hallway. As you look around, you'll see painted signs like "I still remember my name," Lost Ones, and new ink pipes throughout.

When you press on, you'll discover a throne at the center of it all, Joey's own chair, removed from his office. Projector screens around the room play cartoons you'll recognize from the posters around the studio. There will be an audio recording beside the throne.

IT'S SIMPLY AWE—INSPIRING WHAT ONE CAN ACCOMPLISH WITH THEIR OWN HANDS.

A LUMP OF CLAY CAN TURN TO MEANING... IF YOU STRANGLE IT WITH ENOUGH ENTHUSIASM. LOOK WHAT WE'VE BUILT. WE CREATED LIFE ITSELF, HENRY! NOT JUST ON THE SILVER SCREEN, BUT IN THE HEARTS OF THOSE WE ENTERTAINED WITH OUR FANCY MOVING PICTURES. BUT... WHEN THE TICKETS STOPPED SELLING... WHEN THE NEXT BIG THING CAME ALONG... ONLY THE MONSTERS REMAINED... SHADOWS OF THE PAST. BUT YOU CAN SAVE THEM, HENRY! YOU CAN PEEL IT ALL AWAY! YOU SEE, THERE'S ONLY ONE THING BENDY HAS NEVER KNOWN. HE WAS THERE FOR HIS BEGINNING... BUT HE'S NEVER SEEN: THE END.

BEAST BENDY

After the audio recording is complete, you'll see Ink Bendy appear behind the throne. As you watch, Ink Bendy mutates again into Beast Bendy, with atrophied legs, massive claws, and a sharp-toothed smile. You'll need to tread carefully in this final battle—any hit from Bendy brings instant death.

PHASE 1

Escape into a large open maze of hallways. Beast Bendy will run down each corridor, disappearing into the walls. You'll need to dodge, hide, and run from him while you locate four power switches. Flipping these will open a door to a new area.

Tip: Use the Seeing Tool to reveal arrows that will lead you to a path that is best suited for finding the power switches.

PHASE 2

In this new room, you'll need to turn a valve against the wall to your right to activate the next battle. Lure Beast Bendy toward each of the four pipes running from the floor to the ceiling; you must remain at each ink pipe until Beast Bendy tries to attack you. With each attack, a pipe will shatter. When all four pipes are destroyed, Bendy will disappear, and a new exit will open.

PHASE 3

This new exit will lead you back to the throne room. Insert "The End" movie reel into the projector beside the throne to play it. Just as Beast Bendy bares his teeth, the last reel will play. The screen will read:

THE END

Bendy will take one look at it and begin to disintegrate. The room will fill with a bright, white light, and you'll be taken out of Bendy's domain and into Joey Drew's real-world apartment!

JOEY DREW'S APARTMENT

Take your time to explore Joey Drew's apartment. On a shelf to the right of the door you entered through, you'll notice all the objects you placed on pedestals in Chapter 1. A bulletin board to the left of the kitchen doorway contains letters from former employees of the studio, unpaid bills, a notice of bankruptcy, a photograph, and a colored concept sketch of Bendyland. To the right of the kitchen doorway, Joey's drawing table is littered with storyboard panels from different story beats of Chapters 1-5.

Continuing into the kitchen, you'll find Joey himself standing at the kitchen sink, washing dishes and whistling Bendy's song. He'll acknowledge that you have questions. Then he'll say that he has a question of his own: "Who are we, Henry?" Joey will continue.

"IN THE END, WE FOLLOWED TWO DIFFERENT ROADS OF OUR OWN MAKING. YOU! A LOVELY FAMILY... ME... A CROOKED EMPIRE. AND MY ROAD BURNED. I LET OUR CREATIONS BECOME MY LIFE. THE TRUTH IS, YOU WERE ALWAYS SO GOOD AT PUSHING, OLD FRIEND... PUSHING ME TO DO THE RIGHT THING. YOU SHOULD HAVE PUSHED A LITTLE HARDER. HENRY, COME VISIT THE OLD WORKSHOP. THERE'S SOMETHING I WANT TO SHOW YOU."

The calendar date on the wall in the kitchen changes with each playthrough.

Through the door in Joey's apartment, you'll be led back to the beginning of the workshop. After the credits roll, a bonus scene will play. From the kitchen, the camera pans to the opposite wall, where a picture of Bendy, Boris, and Alice hangs. You'll be able to catch a glimpse of Joey's garage through the doorway, which contains the infamous Ink Machine. As you zoom in on the picture, a little girl's voice says, "Tell me another one, Uncle Joey."

Congratulations on your success!
Your Best Pal
Henry Stein

After completing the game, you'll be able to unlock the Seeing Tool in all chapters, as well as bonus content, a new chapter called *The Archives*.

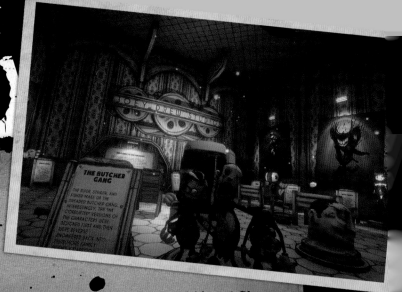

Bonus Content:
WELCOME TO THE ARCHIVES

Bendy and the Ink Machine began when the developer/cartoonist known as theMeatly experimented with bringing a sketched 2-D style into a 3-D world. After turning the idea into a horror game, Chapter 1 of the game was created in a little under a week with a programmer/friend, Mike Mood, and released on February 10, 2017. Much to their surprise, it struck a chord with global indie gamers almost overnight. TheMeatly and Mike Mood decided to drop all other projects to work on Bendy and tell a most unique ink story.

The entire game was completed a chapter at a time in a year and a half by a small but dedicated group of indie developers. Although the concept and story remained as originally intended, the game changed over development as characters and models were refined from their early "thrown-together" versions. This archive is a peek behind the scenes at that process.

Hop up onto the empty pedestal to unlock the "Standing Proud" achievement!

HENRY STEIN

ONCE AN EQUAL BUSINESS PARTNER OF JOEY DREW, HENRY STEIN WAS A TALENTED ANIMATOR AND CHARACTER DESIGNER UNTIL LEAVING THE COMPANY AROUND 1930. HIS PLACE IN JOEY DREW STUDIOS' HISTORY IS SOMEWHAT UNDOCUMENTED, BUT HE IS OFTEN RUMORED TO BE THE TRUE CREATOR BEHIND MANY OF THE STUDIO'S MOST MEMORABLE CHARACTERS.

BETA SEARCHER

EARLY IN DEVELOPMENT, WITH JUST A FEW WEEKS TO CREATE CHAPTER 2, THE BETA SEARCHERS WERE DESIGNED IN RECORD TIME BEFORE BEING FULLY RETOOLED LATER ON. THEY WERE THE FIRST FIGHTING ENEMIES ENCOUNTERED IN THE GAME.

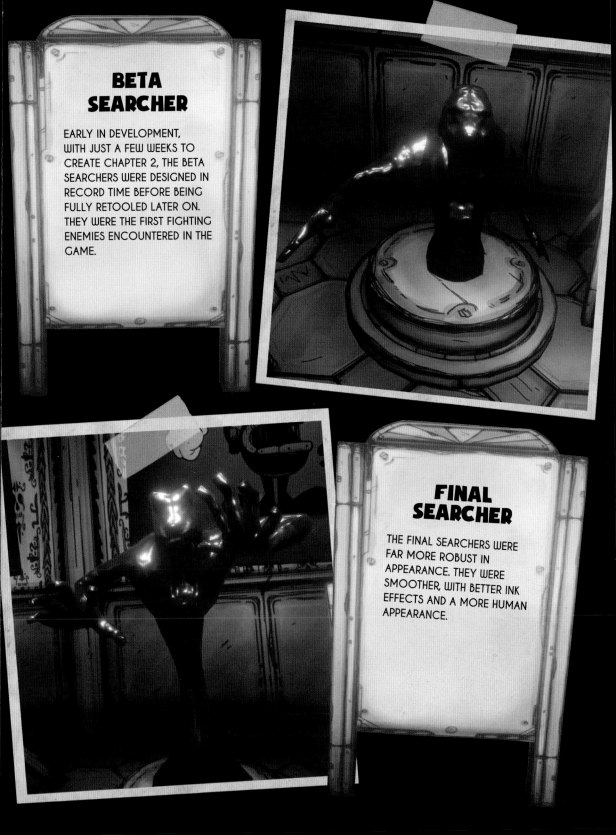

FINAL SEARCHER

THE FINAL SEARCHERS WERE FAR MORE ROBUST IN APPEARANCE. THEY WERE SMOOTHER, WITH BETTER INK EFFECTS AND A MORE HUMAN APPEARANCE.

CONCEPT BENDY

THIS IS THE FIRST VERSION OF BENDY EVER MODELED. IN THE EARLIEST CONCEPTS BENDY WAS MUCH SMALLER (AND CUTER) WITH A FACE THAT SPLIT OPEN TO REVEAL A TERRIFYING MOUTH.

ALPHA BENDY

THIS IS THE ORIGINAL GAME-USED DESIGN OF INK BENDY FROM THE EARLIEST VERSION OF CHAPTER 1. IT IS JOKINGLY REFERRED TO AS "BIRD POOP WITH A SMILE" AMONG THE DEVELOPMENT TEAM.

BETA BENDY

THIS WAS INK BENDY'S FORM UNTIL THE RELEASE OF CHAPTER 4. AT THAT TIME THE GAME RECEIVED A MAJOR VISUAL UPGRADE AND THE TITLE CHARACTER GOT A NEW MODEL AS WELL.

A BENDY

K BENDY'S
L THE RELEASE
R FOUR. A1
THE GAME
MAJOR

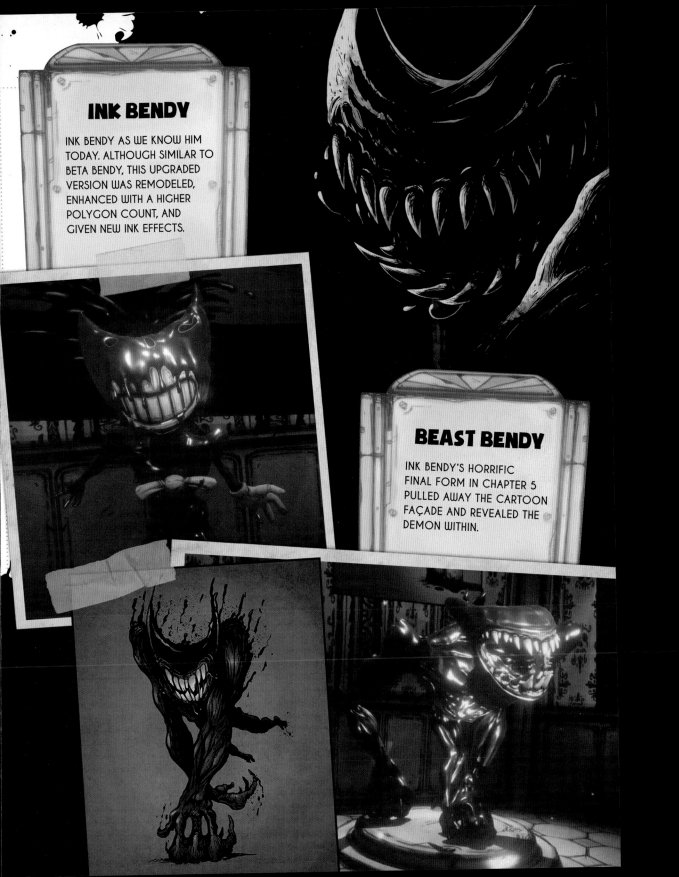

INK BENDY

INK BENDY AS WE KNOW HIM TODAY. ALTHOUGH SIMILAR TO BETA BENDY, THIS UPGRADED VERSION WAS REMODELED, ENHANCED WITH A HIGHER POLYGON COUNT, AND GIVEN NEW INK EFFECTS.

BEAST BENDY

INK BENDY'S HORRIFIC FINAL FORM IN CHAPTER 5 PULLED AWAY THE CARTOON FAÇADE AND REVEALED THE DEMON WITHIN.

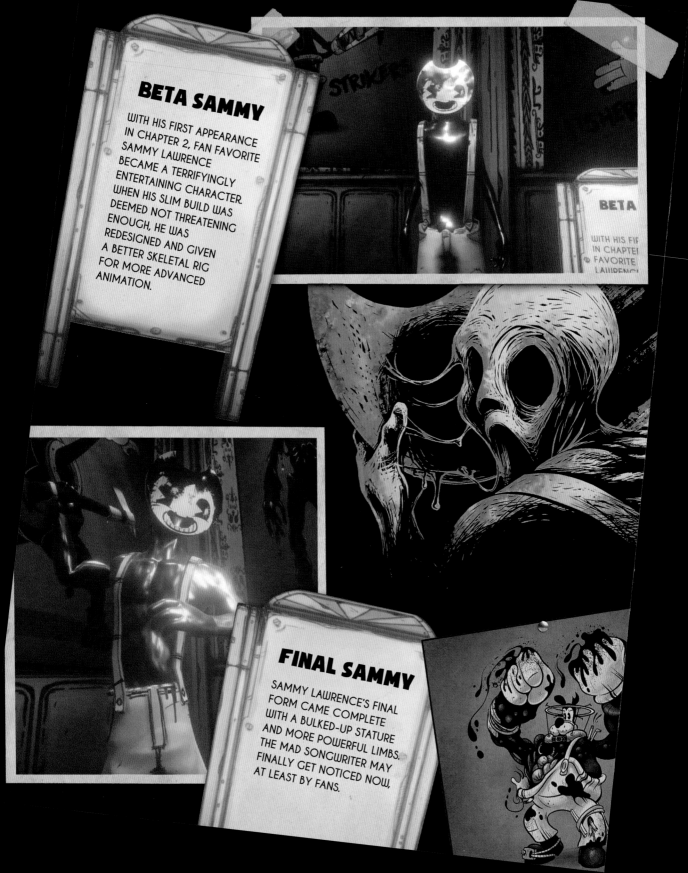

BETA SAMMY

WITH HIS FIRST APPEARANCE
IN CHAPTER 2, FAN FAVORITE
SAMMY LAWRENCE
BECAME A TERRIFYINGLY
ENTERTAINING CHARACTER.
WHEN HIS SLIM BUILD WAS
DEEMED NOT THREATENING
ENOUGH, HE WAS
REDESIGNED AND GIVEN
A BETTER SKELETAL RIG
FOR MORE ADVANCED
ANIMATION.

FINAL SAMMY

SAMMY LAWRENCE'S FINAL
FORM CAME COMPLETE
WITH A BULKED-UP STATURE
AND MORE POWERFUL LIMBS.
THE MAD SONGWRITER MAY
FINALLY GET NOTICED NOW,
AT LEAST BY FANS.

BETA BORIS

"PAPA" WAS THE ORIGINAL
NAME OF THE CHARACTER
THAT EVENTUALLY BECAME
BORIS THE WOLF. THIS EARLY
VERSION WAS RELEASED
WITH CHAPTER 1. HE WAS
QUICKLY REFINED INTO THE
BORIS WE KNOW TODAY
WITH THE RELEASE OF
CHAPTER 2.

BORIS THE WOLF

BORIS THE WOLF, A FRIEND
TO THE END, WAS DESIGNED
USING VARIOUS REFERENCES
FROM CARTOONS OF
THE 1920S. A BLEND OF
WEST COAST AND EAST
COAST ANIMATION
STYLES, THIS SILENT AND
SUPPORTIVE WOLF WON
OVER THE HEARTS OF MANY,
ALTHOUGH AT TIMES HE
WAS A HEADACHE FOR THE
DEVELOPMENT TEAM DUE
TO HIS AI TAKING ON A
MIND OF ITS OWN DURING
PRODUCTION.

BRUTE BORIS

ALICE ANGEL'S MONSTROSITY,
BRUTE BORIS, WAS ONE OF
THE BIGGEST SURPRISES
OF CHAPTER 4. HIS DESIGN
WAS ROUGHLY BASED ON
FRANKENSTEIN'S MONSTER
BUT WITH A MORE UNFINISHED
APPEARANCE. ALICE TOOK
PARTS FROM WITHIN HIM AND
SUBSTITUTED THINGS THAT HIS
BODY IS RAPIDLY REJECTING.

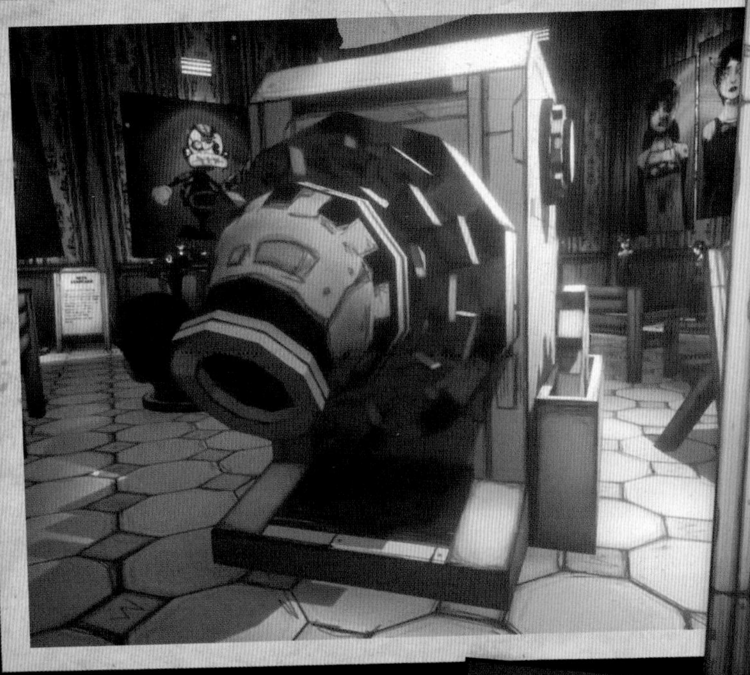

ORIGINAL INK MACHINE

BEFORE A MAJOR VISUAL UPGRADE, THIS VERSION OF THE INK MACHINE WAS THE ONE USED IN THE GAME. MUCH OF THIS MACHINE'S ICONIC, FAN-LOVED DESIGN WAS TRANSLATED INTO THE FINAL VERSION.

THE BUTCHER GANG

THE PIPER, STRIKER, AND FISHER MAKE UP THE DREADED BUTCHER GANG. INTERESTINGLY, THE "INK-CORRUPTED" VERSIONS OF THE CHARACTERS WERE DESIGNED FIRST AND THEN WERE REVERSE ENGINEERED BACK INTO THEIR MORE FAMILY-FRIENDLY CARTOON FORMS.

STRIKERS

PIPERS

FISHERS

LIAR

BERTRUM
PIEDMONT
HEAD

TWISTED
ALICE

ALICE

SECRET MESSAGES IN CHAPTERS 1–4

Once you've completed the main story, you'll unlock the Seeing Tool to use in Chapters 1–4. Hundreds of secret messages exist in these chapters, but some of the best appear below.

- Chapter 1, entrance hallway: Tally marks line the walls.

- Chapter 1, Henry's desktop: "He was born here."

- Chapter 1, toilet in the Animation Department: "Can I get a little privacy?"

- Chapter 1, floor in front of the Ink Machine: "There *never* was a choice."

- Chapter 1, in front of the sacrificed Boris: "She's heartless."

- Chapter 1, radio room: "Listening and always watching"

- Chapter 1, theMeatly's room: "Devilishly handsome"

- Chapter 1, room after the fall, where you get the axe: "Joey lied to us."

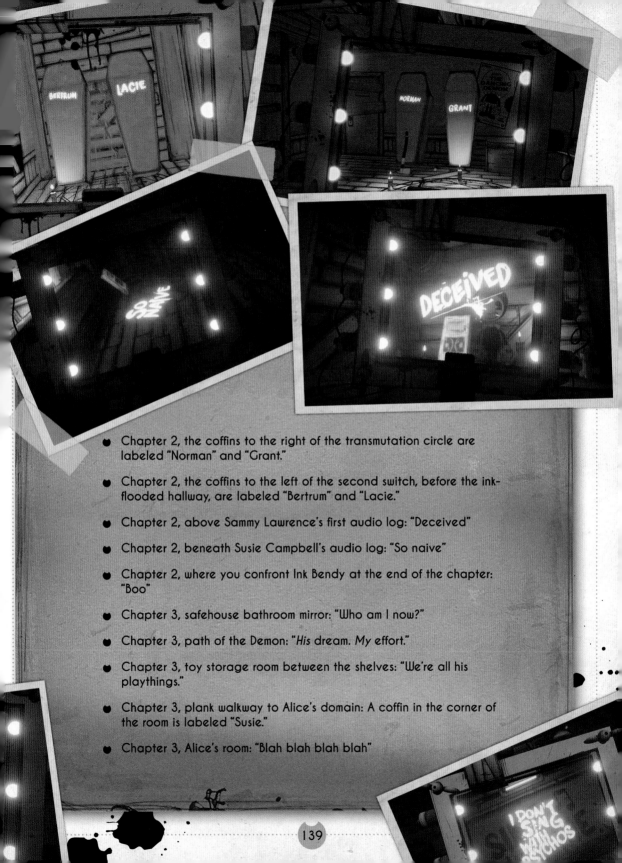

- Chapter 2, the coffins to the right of the transmutation circle are labeled "Norman" and "Grant."

- Chapter 2, the coffins to the left of the second switch, before the ink-flooded hallway, are labeled "Bertrum" and "Lacie."

- Chapter 2, above Sammy Lawrence's first audio log: "Deceived"

- Chapter 2, beneath Susie Campbell's audio log: "So naive"

- Chapter 2, where you confront Ink Bendy at the end of the chapter: "Boo"

- Chapter 3, safehouse bathroom mirror: "Who am I now?"

- Chapter 3, path of the Demon: "*His* dream. *My* effort."

- Chapter 3, toy storage room between the shelves: "We're all his playthings."

- Chapter 3, plank walkway to Alice's domain: A coffin in the corner of the room is labeled "Susie."

- Chapter 3, Alice's room: "Blah blah blah blah"

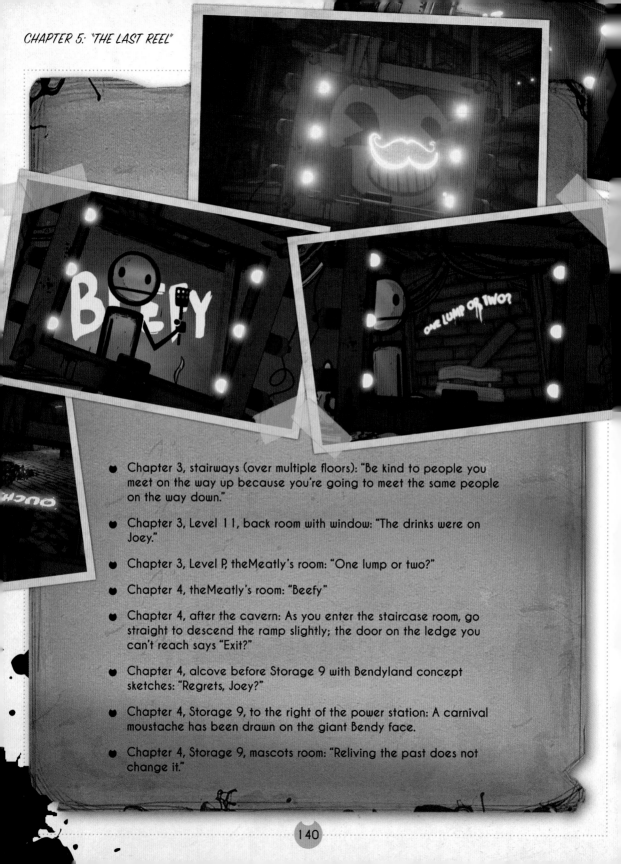

- Chapter 3, stairways (over multiple floors): "Be kind to people you meet on the way up because you're going to meet the same people on the way down."

- Chapter 3, Level 11, back room with window: "The drinks were on Joey."

- Chapter 3, Level P, theMeatly's room: "One lump or two?"

- Chapter 4, theMeatly's room: "Beefy"

- Chapter 4, after the cavern: As you enter the staircase room, go straight to descend the ramp slightly; the door on the ledge you can't reach says "Exit?"

- Chapter 4, alcove before Storage 9 with Bendyland concept sketches: "Regrets, Joey?"

- Chapter 4, Storage 9, to the right of the power station: A carnival moustache has been drawn on the giant Bendy face.

- Chapter 4, Storage 9, mascots room: "Reliving the past does not change it."

- Chapter 4, Research & Design, under the Lost One's cage: "Please don't cry."

- Chapter 4, Research & Design, on the box beside the animatronic: "It never moves."

- Chapter 4, Attractions, Bertrum Piedmont's room, under the "Buddy Boris Railway" poster: "Time wounds all heels."

- Chapter 4, Maintenance, first floor beside Joey's audio log: "That's the Joey I knew."

- Chapter 5, Henry's prison in the hideout: The notes above Henry's cot include three notes in a different handwriting style ("ink," "spoon," "escape"). Who left these?

- Chapter 5, office of Joey Drew, above the door: "Who is the man behind the monster?"

- Chapter 5, after Tom and Alice rejoin you in the Film Vault, look through your viewfinder at Tom; if you gave Boris a bone in Chapter 3, a bone will be visible in Tom's mouth here.

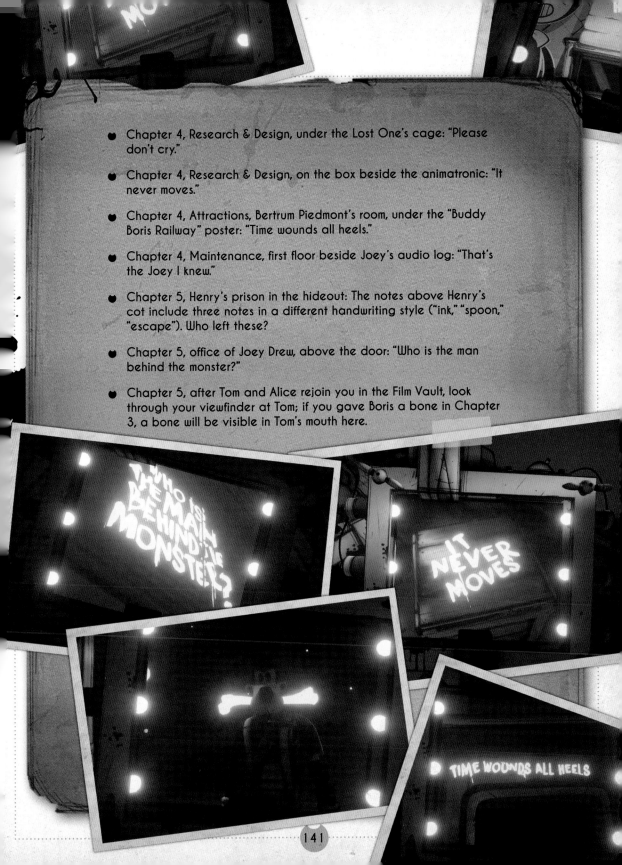

PART II

WELCOME TO THE STUDIO!

Now that you've gotten through your first week, it's time to take a closer look at Joey Drew Studios. In this section, you'll learn about the company's employee benefits as well as incentives, rewards, and organizational charts.

Mister Drew,

I'm happy to share our top-secret Briar Label Bacon Soup recipe with you! Please be sure to keep this somewhere safe though. We'd be ruined if our competitors found out there's no beef in the soup.

- Wilfred Briar

BRIAR LABEL BACON SOUP

INGREDIENTS

- 1 lb. premium Canadian bacon
- ¾ cup chopped onion
- ¾ cup peeled, diced carrots
- ¾ cup diced celery
- 4 cups peeled, diced potatoes
- 4 tbsps butter
- 3 cups chicken broth
- ¼ cup flour
- 2 cups cheddar cheese
- 1 cup milk
- ½ cup heavy cream
- 1 tsp salt
- 1 tsp pepper

Kids, ask an adult to help you!

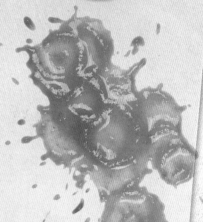

INSTRUCTIONS

1. Using 1 tbsp of butter, sauté onions, carrots, and celery in a large soup pot until tender. Add chopped bacon to the pot and cook until crispy.

2. Add broth and potatoes to your soup pot, bringing it to a boil. Reduce heat, keeping the soup on a simmer. Cook ten minutes, or until potatoes are tender.

3. Combine 3 tbsps of butter with the flour in a skillet, cooking for roughly five minutes, or until bubbly. Add this to the soup pot, and bring it to a boil once again. Reduce heat, simmering soup for another 3-5 minutes.

4. Reduce heat to low. Stir heavy cream, milk, cheese, salt, and pepper into the soup pot, cooking until cheese is melted.

ANIMATION DEPARTMENT ORGANIZATIONAL CHART

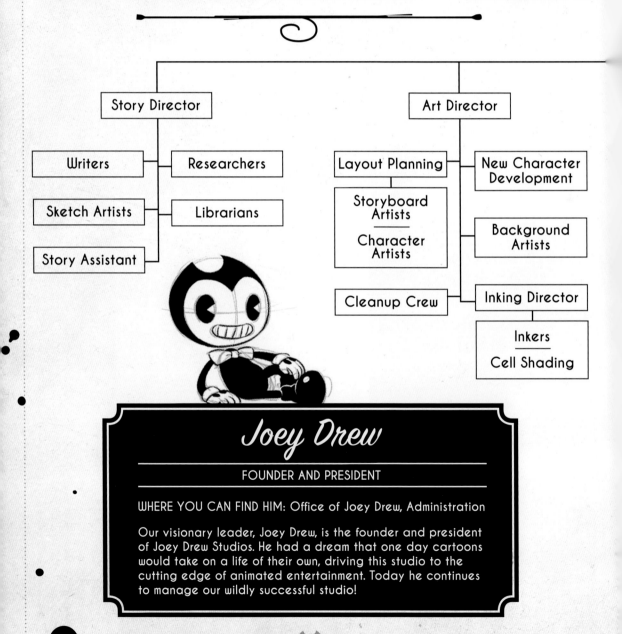

Story Director
- Writers
- Researchers
- Sketch Artists
- Librarians
- Story Assistant

Art Director
- Layout Planning
- New Character Development
- Storyboard Artists — Character Artists
- Background Artists
- Cleanup Crew
- Inking Director
- Inkers — Cell Shading

Joey Drew

FOUNDER AND PRESIDENT

WHERE YOU CAN FIND HIM: Office of Joey Drew, Administration

Our visionary leader, Joey Drew, is the founder and president of Joey Drew Studios. He had a dream that one day cartoons would take on a life of their own, driving this studio to the cutting edge of animated entertainment. Today he continues to manage our wildly successful studio!

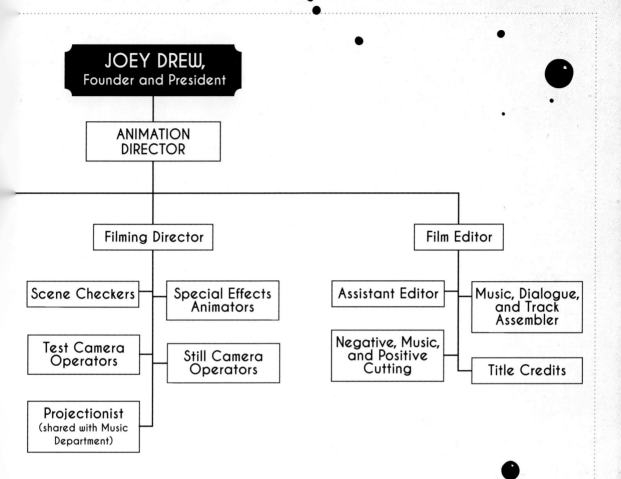

JOEY DREW,
Founder and President

ANIMATION DIRECTOR

Filming Director

Scene Checkers

Special Effects Animators

Test Camera Operators

Still Camera Operators

Projectionist
(shared with Music Department)

Film Editor

Assistant Editor

Music, Dialogue, and Track Assembler

Negative, Music, and Positive Cutting

Title Credits

Norman Polk

PROJECTIONIST

WHERE YOU CAN FIND HIM: Anywhere!

Norman is the cinematic expert at Joey Drew Studios. A bit of a recluse, Norman much prefers the quiet of the theater to the hubbub of the bull pen, but he's happy to help with any questions you may have, should you manage to find him.

MUSIC DEPARTMENT ORGANIZATIONAL CHART

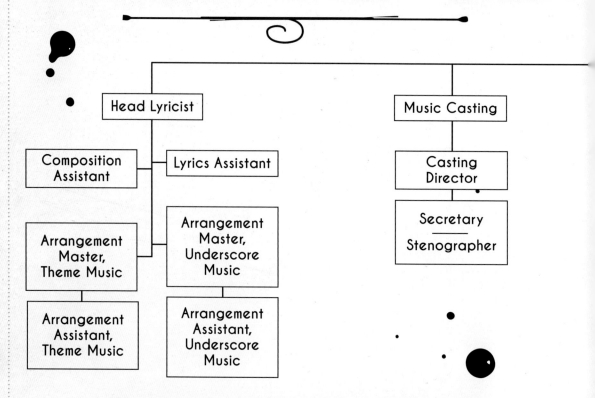

Head Lyricist

Music Casting

Composition Assistant

Lyrics Assistant

Casting Director

Arrangement Master, Theme Music

Arrangement Master, Underscore Music

Secretary — Stenographer

Arrangement Assistant, Theme Music

Arrangement Assistant, Underscore Music

Sammy Lawrence

MUSIC DIRECTOR

WHERE YOU CAN FIND HIM: Office of Music Director, Music Department

Sammy Lawrence is the company's music director, responsible for all the audio in our cartoons, including theme songs, scores, voice recordings, and sound effects.

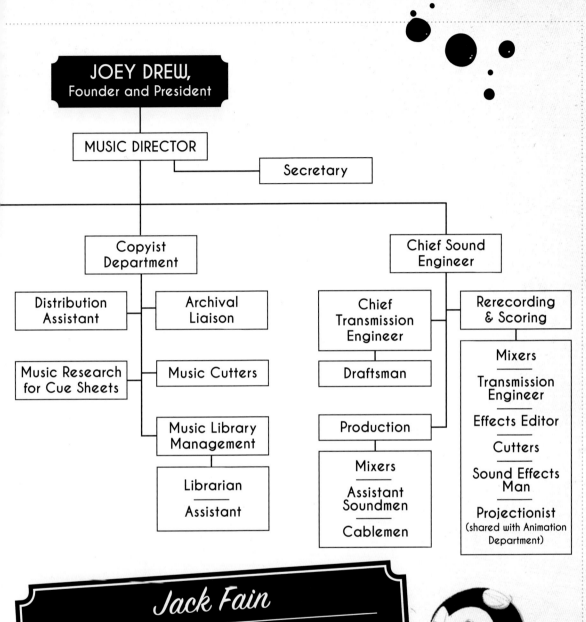

JOEY DREW,
Founder and President

MUSIC DIRECTOR

Secretary

Copyist Department

Distribution Assistant

Archival Liaison

Music Research for Cue Sheets

Music Cutters

Music Library Management

Librarian
Assistant

Chief Sound Engineer

Chief Transmission Engineer

Draftsman

Production

Mixers
Assistant Soundmen
Cablemen

Rerecording & Scoring

Mixers
Transmission Engineer
Effects Editor
Cutters
Sound Effects Man
Projectionist
(shared with Animation Department)

Jack Fain

LYRICIST

WHERE YOU CAN FIND HIM: Music Department

Jack Fain is the head lyricist at Joey Drew Studios, meaning he writes the words to all the theme songs in our cartoons. Jack reports to Sammy Lawrence, and can usually be spotted hanging around the recording studio in his bowler hat.

ACCOUNTING & FINANCE DEPARTMENT
ORGANIZATIONAL CHART

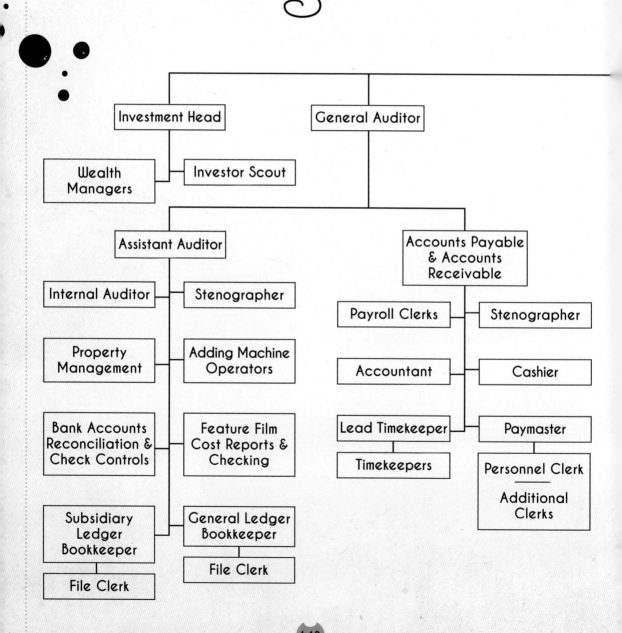

Investment Head

General Auditor

Wealth Managers — Investor Scout

Assistant Auditor

Accounts Payable & Accounts Receivable

Internal Auditor — Stenographer

Payroll Clerks — Stenographer

Property Management — Adding Machine Operators

Accountant — Cashier

Bank Accounts Reconciliation & Check Controls — Feature Film Cost Reports & Checking

Lead Timekeeper — Paymaster

Timekeepers

Subsidiary Ledger Bookkeeper — General Ledger Bookkeeper

Personnel Clerk

Additional Clerks

File Clerk

File Clerk

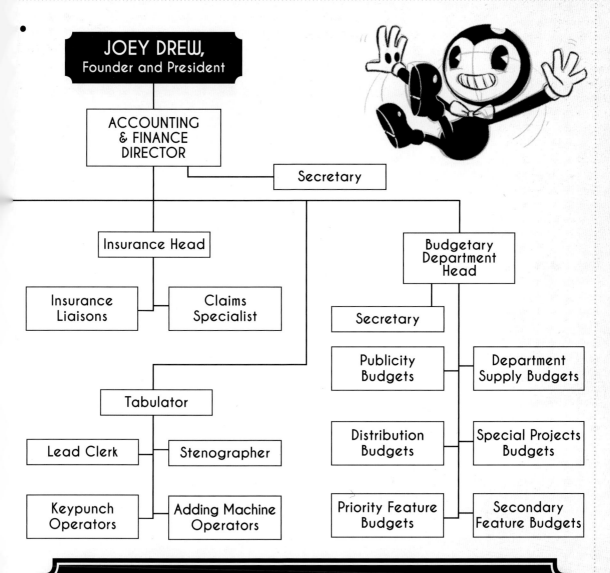

JOEY DREW,
Founder and President

ACCOUNTING & FINANCE DIRECTOR

Secretary

Insurance Head

Insurance Liaisons

Claims Specialist

Tabulator

Lead Clerk

Stenographer

Keypunch Operators

Adding Machine Operators

Budgetary Department Head

Secretary

Publicity Budgets

Department Supply Budgets

Distribution Budgets

Special Projects Budgets

Priority Feature Budgets

Secondary Feature Budgets

Grant Cohen

ACCOUNTING & FINANCE DIRECTOR

WHERE YOU CAN FIND HIM: Accounting & Finance Offices, Level S

Although Grant isn't exactly a creative dreamer, he does dream . . . in numbers. As the Accounting & Finance director, Grant is able to balance the company's checkbooks, funds, and make sure everything is staying afloat. He reports directly to Joey Drew.

ADMINISTRATION AND SPECIAL PROJECTS DEPARTMENTS ORGANIZATIONAL CHART

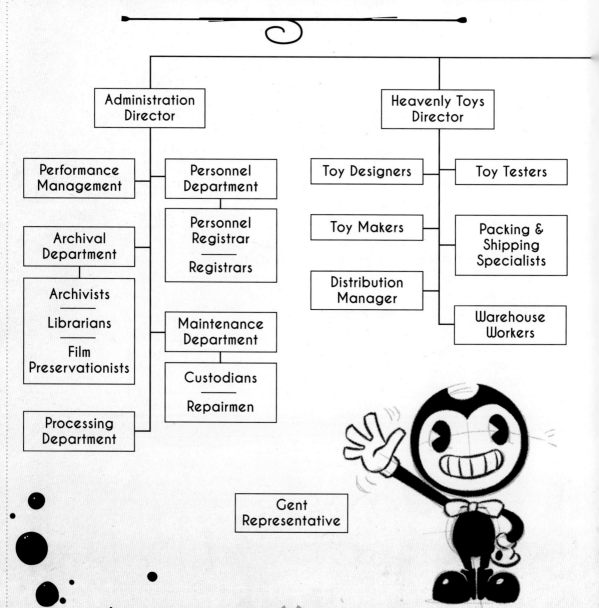

Administration Director

- Performance Management
- Personnel Department
  - Personnel Registrar
    - Registrars
- Archival Department
  - Archivists
    - Librarians
    - Film Preservationists
- Maintenance Department
  - Custodians
    - Repairmen
- Processing Department

Heavenly Toys Director

- Toy Designers
- Toy Testers
- Toy Makers
- Packing & Shipping Specialists
- Distribution Manager
- Warehouse Workers

Gent Representative

Organization Chart

JOEY DREW,
Founder and President

Special Projects Director, Bendyland

Lead Engineer

Construction Manager

Assistant Engineers, Games

Assistant Engineers, Attractions

Assistant Engineers, Construction

Warehouse Workers

Assemblers

Machinists

Site Manager

Financial Planner

Materials Specialist

Vendor Liaison

Budget Manager

Shawn Flynn

TOY MAKER

WHERE YOU CAN FIND HIM: Heavenly Toys Room

Shawn Flynn is a toy maker with our subsidiary, Heavenly Toys. He uses our machinery to create toys that feel on brand for Bendy and the other cartoon characters.

Lacie Benton

ENGINEER, SPECIAL PROJECTS, BENDYLAND

WHERE YOU CAN FIND HER: Bendyland Research & Design

Lacie works alongside Special Projects director Bertie Piedmont to help bring the Bendyland dream to life.

Wally Franks

JANITOR

WHERE YOU CAN FIND HIM: Throughout the Studio

Wally is a janitor within our Maintenance Department. In addition to cleaning up general employee messes, Wally's role has recently expanded to assist with malfunctions of Gent machinery.

Thomas Connor

GENT REPRESENTATIVE

WHERE YOU CAN FIND HIM: Throughout the Studio

Thomas Connor is a representative for Gent Corporation, which has produced much of the plumbing and new technology around our studio. He can often be seen milling about the studio, making sure the piping is running as it should. While Thomas isn't strictly an employee of the studio, he is like family to us!

What We Expect of You

We hate to invoke the threatening tone of "Rules and Regulations," but we also want to make sure you know what's expected of you and your work for our wonderful company.

Joey Drew Studios hires strictly the best, and that's all we expect of you—the best. Working hours at the studio are set for 8:00 AM to 5:00 PM, but overtime is frequently required to meet our rigorous deadlines. Overtime will be needed after normal studio hours and on weekends during our high-output periods of the year. A reminder that if you are part of our Animation, Music, or Special Projects Departments, you are likely salaried and thus ineligible for overtime pay. You can avoid unpaid overtime work requirements by completing projects to the highest standards in a timely manner.

Remember: Mister Drew is listening and always watching! Tardiness, personal phone calls, lengthy lunch breaks, and time spent socializing will not go unnoticed and could result in disciplinary action.

We observe a casual dress policy at the studio to foster an atmosphere conducive to creativity, but please keep in mind that business attire may be required for high-level meetings. We ask that you convene with your supervisor if you are unsure of the dress code for a particular event.

Mister Drew built this studio through perseverance and imagination, but also through collaboration and friendship. Poor attitudes, negativity, and gossip distract from our sacred mission to bring joy to the children of the world. Termination will be considered if such behavior becomes prevalent in your work, so be sure to put on a smile at all times!

Your First Day at the Studio

The morning of your first day, please report directly to Administration for new employee processing. Your first morning will be spent navigating the labyrinth of Administration offices, as we set you up in our various systems of record keeping.

First stop: Registration! Our Personnel Registrar will collect Packet 12A from you. As you know, this packet includes information about your position, salary, contact information, and employment history. This packet will start your file at our company, to which will ultimately be added performance evaluations, any merit raises/promotions, and (though we hope not) any disciplinary actions taken against you. At this point,

you will also be issued your own identification badge, which you will need to show to reception as you enter and exit the studio.

Next stop: Payroll! Be sure to bring your forms from Packet 524B so Payroll can process your information and set up your paychecks. Here you will also meet the Paymaster. As you might imagine, the Paymaster is responsible for overseeing and delivering your paycheck. Every other Friday is payday, when the Paymaster travels to each department to hand-deliver checks. If you miss the Paymaster during his rounds, you will need to travel to Administration to pick up your paycheck from him directly. Paychecks must be collected in person; delivery to your desk is not permitted.

Finally: Orientation! New Hire Orientation will take you downstairs to the Archives on Level S. Here you'll be treated to a brief history of Joey Drew Studios and our many accomplishments. If you're lucky, Mister Drew himself might even stop by to say hello!

After Orientation, you will be taken to your department and handed over to your supervisor. Take a minute to say hello to your new teammates as they welcome you to the Joey Drew family. Then it's time to get to work!

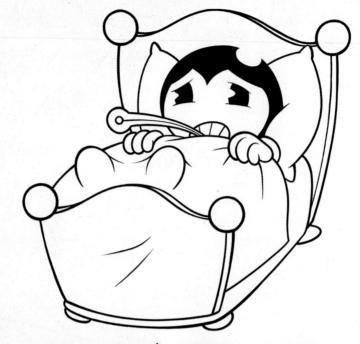

Health Benefits

Eat some bad bacon? Feel a little nauseated? Come down with a case of . . . well, it's best we don't know. Don't worry, your employer has you covered. Joey Drew Studios is proud to offer a comprehensive health benefits package limited to free, no-charge visits to the studio's state-of-the-art Infirmary. Employees who feel sick need not stay home; simply stop by the Infirmary on your way to your desk. There you'll find a menagerie of treatments and medicines to help you feel better and back to work in no time—no pesky recovery time required! Qualified medical staff are on-site several days each month to consult with you about your needs.

In the unlikely event that you should require sick leave, you may petition for paid sick leave benefits by checking in with Administration. There you can pick up Packets 259B, 1027A, 40L, and 723D. Fill out these

forms in triplicate and be sure to submit them to Administration along with a detailed letter from your doctor within two days of absence. If your forms are approved, your pay will be included in your next paycheck.

Besides your health, we also want to make sure you're doing what you can to protect your safety on the job. Be sure to hold the handrails as you ascend and descend the stairways, follow all posted protocols for interacting with equipment, and report any unsafe working conditions to our janitor, Wally Franks. Should an accident occur on the job, please file a report with Administration within twenty-four hours. From there, the condition and any necessary medical leave can be addressed.

We know that, above all else, your heart is in the work we do here. Excessive absences don't benefit yourself or your fellow employees, who still have to complete your department's collective work on time. For this reason, employees are only eligible for five days of paid leave per year. Absences above that number—due to illness or otherwise—will likely result in immediate termination.

Holidays and Vacation Time

Dreams don't happen at random. They come from cultured, happy employees!

To this end, we are thrilled to offer the following holidays off for our employees, noting of course that service the day before and after the holiday is expected: New Year's Day, Memorial Day, July Fourth, Labor Day, Thanksgiving, Christmas.

In some animation studios we will not name, employees are given *paid* vacation time, and while that all sounds fine and dandy, we must ask: Why, in Bendy's good name, would anyone need to take a vacation from their job unless they *hated* it?

Once your company loyalty is proven with five years of continuous service, Joey Drew Studios is thrilled to offer five days of unpaid vacation time, with which we hope you'll take your family on a wholesome, well-earned trip to our Bendyland amusement park when it's complete. We hope these days away from your job give you time to really appreciate it and the inherent value in a hard day's work.

Until you've built up this trust with the company, take a look at some of our wonderful "studio vacations" below. If you catch yourself dreaming of faraway vistas, consider one of these more practical alternatives!

- When you're thinking about Bora Bora . . . Draw your own beach, and hang it up right at your workspace. A big inspiration for "The Dancing Demon" came from our animators dreaming of Hawaii!

- When you're thinking about Mexico . . . Let Mr. Franks tell you about the time he thought he ate some tasty churros but they turned out to be . . . well, we'll let him tell you.

- When you're thinking about Paris . . . Joey Drew currently holds the office record for highest tower of Bacon Soup cans. Can you beat him? Try your best, and don't forget to dispose of your cans in the salvage bin to help with the war effort!

- When you're dreaming about Miami . . . Isn't Florida under sea level? You can be too—just bust off one of the valves in Utility Shaft 9! (This is office humor. You really shouldn't do this, as it's very disruptive.)

Employee Rewards

There are many additional employee rewards available to you while working at Joey Drew Studios. Find out all our animation studio has to offer below!

EMPLOYEE OF THE MONTH

This is a new initiative that we'll be starting soon: Employee of the Month. How it works is simple. Joey Drew was the first employee, so he'll be the first employee of the month. If anyone is better than him, they get to be employee of the month. So far no one's usurped Joey . . . but maybe that will change with you!

JOEY DREW
EMPLOYEE OF THE MONTH

FREE TOILET PAPER

Worried you'd have to bring your own toilet paper to the studio? Think again! The bathrooms at Joey Drew Studios are stocked with all the TP your little heart could ever desire. And it's two-ply too. Now that's love! Just don't use too much. Mr. Franks has enough to do.

HOLIDAY BONUSES

The holidays are time for family . . . and when you're here, you're part of Joey's family. To thank you for all of your hard work, we are pleased to reward our employees the opportunity to earn overtime by working Christmas, so you can celebrate our work with the ones you love most—Bendy, Boris the Wolf, and Alice Angel!

HOLIDAY PARTIES

In addition to our Halloween party (which has spooky stories, candied bacon, and a costume contest), we also have various parties throughout the year. We celebrate Bendy's birthday (the day Bendy was created—there's devil's food cake!), Alice Angel's birthday (angel food cake!), Boris's birthday (bacon! Mm, salty), and, of course, Joey Drew's birthday (everyone stays overtime to wish Joey a happy birthday!).

Bendyland

Amusement parks are all the craze these days. It seems like they're everywhere! Fortunately, Bendy fans will have only one themed amusement park to visit from now on—Bendyland. Joey Drew had the fashionable idea at dinner one day, and the endeavor was launched in 1940 with the help of famed amusement park designer Bertrum Piedmont. Mr. Piedmont was hired immediately after Joey had the idea, bringing with him an impressive resume cobbled together from forty years designing parks for various clients.

Bendyland will be home to a number of fantastical and wonderful Bendy-themed attractions, including Light Land, Big Land, Dark Land, and Tiny Land.

Employees of Joey Drew Studios will soon get to reap all the wonderful benefits of Bendyland. In addition to a free lifetime pass* (well, as long as you stay employed here, but that'll be a lifetime!), you also get up to four guest passes, should you somehow mingle with people who aren't your direct coworkers. You'll also get a 40 percent discount to use on your purchases.**

We're thrilled to share more information about Bendyland with you in the coming months!

* The Bendyland Employee Pass is not valid on New Year's Day, Groundhog Day, Mardi Gras, Ash Wednesday, Valentine's Day, Chinese New Year, Purim, Holi, St. Patrick's Day, Good Friday, Easter Sunday, Easter Monday, Passover, Tax Day, Cinco de Mayo, Mother's Day, Ramadan, Memorial Day, Flag Day, Father's Day, Eid al-Fitr, Independence Day, Labor Day, Rosh Hashanah, Yom Kippur, Sukkot, Columbus Day, Navaratri, Halloween, All Saints' Day, Veterans Day, The Day Before Thanksgiving, Thanksgiving, Thanksgiving Weekend, or all of the month of December. Also not valid during work hours or blackout dates.

** Employee discount is limited to a one-time use only. Discount voucher not valid on toys, food, apparel, bedding, churros that aren't being used as food but are being used as—well, ask Mr. Franks—books, stationery, cold weather gear, hot weather gear, drinks, jewelry, Bacon Soup, or key chains.

Directions:

Those Employee of the Month awards don't come cheap. You're working late and need coffee. So, first, you'll need to head downstairs.

New Objective:

LOCATE THE ELEVATOR

The elevator is just down the hall, through the Arch Gate offices to the right. Wouldn't you know it, the door leading to the elevator is locked! Good thing you have your own key, only it's back at your desk.

RETRIEVE YOUR OFFICE KEYS

Head back to your desk, where you'll easily find the key. You'll see a Bendy floor-standee on the way, though it's been removed on the way back. That's odd.

TIME TO REFLECT ACHIEVEMENT
Check the mirror on the wall in Audrey's room five times, be sure to stand close. After the fifth time you're in for a surprise . . .

AVID WORKER ACHIEVEMENT
Stay at your desk for 20 minutes, do not touch a thing, before allowing Audrey to stand up. This Achievement/Trophy also unlocks a secret ending.

DID YOU SEE THAT? ACHIEVEMENT
After using the Office Key to open the locked door, summon the elevator, then search for three balls to drop into the bucket at the end of the next hallway.

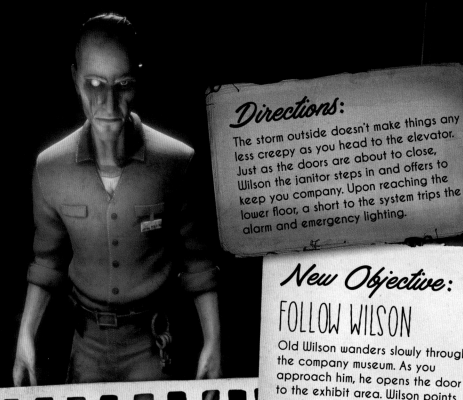

Directions:

The storm outside doesn't make things any less creepy as you head to the elevator. Just as the doors are about to close, Wilson the janitor steps in and offers to keep you company. Upon reaching the lower floor, a short to the system trips the alarm and emergency lighting.

New Objective:
FOLLOW WILSON

Old Wilson wanders slowly through the company museum. As you approach him, he opens the door to the exhibit area. Wilson points out that there should be something on each of the pedestals and asks that you go and find them while he attends to the power.

SEARCH FOR THE EXHIBITS

There are six exhibits in all. You won't need to search far or for very long:

The wrench is on the throw switch as you leave (or enter) the exhibit room.

The gear is inside the wall-mounted green cabinet with a gear painted on it.

You'll grab the Bendy plushy from its perch on a chair in the corner of the room.

Beneath the black-and-white photograph of Joey Drew you'll find a pot of ink.

A *Bendy Sing Along* vinyl is on a record player, on the shelf by the window.

Joey Drew's book *The Illusion of Living* is right there on the bookshelf.

Directions:

Before disturbing Wilson, who's hard at work on the power, place all six exhibits to match the pictures on their pedestals. Job done, now you can check on Wilson's progress.

New Objective:

TURN ON THE POWER

Wilson asks you to pull the switch marked "Flow." His response is worrying, saying, "Oh, Audrey, the things you've set in motion." As the room floods with ink, Wilson says you're "going home," which is ominous. Ink is rising fast. Wilson drags you under . . . to your death.

ESCAPE THE STUDIO

After you regain consciousness, you notice your hands look and feel strange, and the line-drawn room is equally unnerving. To escape the studio, you first need two ladder rungs from the right-hand desk drawer.

BE CURIOUS

Always search lockers, barrels, cupboards, and crates, where you'll often find items such as Gent parts, Gent batteries, and more.

STUDIO MEMO

THE BEGINNING

Every great story begins in mystery. Although things may be dark at the start, the truth will illuminate your way. Don't be afraid of who you are. Fear only what you may become, and banish it away.

—Your Best Pal

STUDIO MEMO

LET'S TALK

Joey,

Jack and I have been wondering if you could meet with us considering the current situation? We have been with you for many years and we feel we have contributed to the success of Bendy in the past.

Our interest is purely in keeping this company strong. We just want to help however we can. Let's talk.

—Sammy Lawrence

STUDIO MEMO

GENT PROPERTY

To: Grant Cohen, accounting:

Please inform Mr. Drew that despite his insistence that the rumors of Joey Drew Studios going bankrupt are untrue, I want to remind him that if his studio does indeed fail, all equipment and experiments produced through our partnership, by contract, belong to the Gent Corporation. We will reclaim these assets forcibly if necessary.

—Alan Gray

Directions:

On the desk with the ladder rungs is "The Beginning—Your Best Pal" memo. Above the desk, inside the cabinet, is the "Gent Property—Alan Gray" memo. Before climbing the ladder, check the broken pipe to find *The Illusion of Living* book.

At the top of the ladder is a "Hard Times—Telly Waster" memo resting on a table there, beside a tiny music box (try giving the key a turn). After ducking into the next corridor, you'll spy the "Let's Talk—Sammy Lawrence" memo on a barrel, just across from the hiding place. Then, as you follow the flooded pathway, another memo, "It Is Close—Unknown," is on top of a crate.

Just after you pass through a gate that slowly opens, prepare for your first jump scare of the journey as a Piper hangs down from a hatch in the ceiling!

STUDIO MEMO

HARD TIMES

Geez! You'd think I was drowning kittens the way these people are lookin' at me! I've never seen such disappointment in a person's eyes.

But this is the way of things, if management can't pay their bills, then the bank takes the goodies back. Still, it does break me a bit knowing how much I loved them old cartoons this place used to make. Oh well! Times change. Life moves on.

—Telly Waster

THE INK DRIPS. DARKNESS HAS SPREAD THROUGHOUT THIS STUDIO. THE REACHING SHADOWS CREEP AROUND YOU. SOMETHING HUNGERS FOR YOUR CORRUPTE FLESH. IT IS CLOSE. SO VERY CLOSE

IT STRAINS TO GRAB YOU, CHOKE YO FROM BEHIND. YOU WILL FEEL ITS BREATH UPON YOUR NEC

IT IS CLOSE.

Directions:

Among the items strewn along these passageways, you'll find a desk upon which you find the first audio Log: "End of an Era—Nathan Arch." In the cabinet above is a baseball, which is the first memory, and next to that a Gent battery. You see, it is always worth checking the cabinets.

Your bid to escape the studio continues, climbing a crumbling wall and on to a Security Override switch opposite two lockers. Once that switch is flipped, you might feel the urge to run! Be careful and keep an eye on your stamina. At last, a place that looks like somewhere: Heavenly Toys? You'll find the memo "Better Things—Shawn Flynn" here, in a desk drawer to the right, opposite another desk with a Gent battery inside.

Voice of
NATHAN ARCH

I just received the call. Joey Drew is dead.

What a quiet end to an extraordinary life. Last I heard he was staying in some cramped apartment downtown. You could practically hear the rats through the telephone when he called me last April. In spite of that, old Joey sounded quite happy when last we spoke.

More like the excited, hopeful young man I knew once upon a time. Ah, well, farewell my friend. What will become of your creations now?

STUDIO MEMO

BETTER THINGS

As the winds are changin' around here, I'm asking meself, Shawn, what are you doin'? There's a whole world out there! Places to see! A family to spend me days with!

This here job is just a job. I'll have others like it. No worry there. But the important thing is: we should remember to live. I think it's time I did just that.

—Shawn Flynn

New Objective:

RUN AND HIDE

A switch at the top of the stairs short circuits when pulled. That's nothing compared to the shock at the nearby wall, where a Piper is waiting. You'll need to make a run for it and hide in the Little Miracle Station, across from the fountain. No, it isn't quite over yet . . .

FIND SOME FOOD

When you're low on health, you'll need to eat. While hunting for a bite—hope you like Bacon Soup—a mysterious young woman, Allison, surprises you. She talks of Searchers, Pipers, her pet wolf . . . It's a lot! But most importantly: Stay away from the Ink Demon!

Directions:

Before heading left at the top of the broken wall, pick up the "Be Careful—Your Best Pal" memo from the stool, then head right to find the "Beast in Chains—Unknown" memo in a desk drawer. Also at the far end of this route is a flight of stairs, leading to another wall, above which you'll find the "Hardly Working—Angus Newman" audio log next to an old radio.

STUDIO MEMO

BE CAREFUL

Around here, it's just best to stay out of sight.

Don't ever go running into some place if you don't know what's in there! If you attack a problem head-on, you're going to find yourself in trouble. And that's just foolish!

You gotta watch, listen, and—when the time is right—push forward.

—Your Best Pal

CHAPTER ONE
"DRAWN TO DARKNESS"

Voice of
ANGUS NEWMAN

Heh! Double quota that Mister Flynn says! Ha! Double! Why, I haven't even pulled a full day's work in that old toy assembly line in some four years, and I don't intend on starting now.

I've got my corner, my sipping little canteen, and I do just fine. Double quota. Ha, I ain't even done half in months! Oh, but they won't fire me. No, sir! Place this big, no one knows what everyone else is doing. Hehe.

So I'll turn up my radio, put my feet up, and count the holes in my socks. Five o'clock comes easy around here! Hehe, buddy!

A NEW TERROR HAS DESCENDED INTO OUR LIVES. THIS MAN NAMED **WILSON.**

EVER SINCE, OUR WORLD FEELS STRAINED, LIKE A **GREAT BEAST** HELD IN CHAINS. THE **INK DEMON** HASN'T BEEN SEEN IN A LONG TIME. MANY OF US REFUSE TO BELIEVE HE'S REALLY GONE.

BUT, WHAT DOES IT MATTER? DOWN HERE, WE'RE ALL **SINNERS.** CHILDREN OF THE **MACHINE** ALL HAVE **THE DEMON IN OUR INKY BLOOD.**

Voice of
DALE LITTLE

Yeah, so those Gent Corporation boys are kinda strange.

Every time I come back to work, they've put in even more'a them pointless gadgets. Last week, they built some kind of, I dunno, electrical towers over near Animation Alley. This week, they added security codes for opening doors. Geez, what kind of work do they think we do here, anyways? Last I checked, we make toys and silly cartoons. I mean, this ain't Fort Knox! You know what I mean? Now it's my job to look over these shipping invoices AND remember a bunch'a random numbers? Yeah, NO FREAKIN' THANK YOU! I'm just going to record the door code here so I don't forget it. Alright: The code is 4 . . . 5 . . . 1 . . .451. And if, uh, Mister Drew or Mister Gray asks, you didn't hear it from me. 'kay?

New Objective:
ESCAPE THE STUDIO

Your only way forward is up that broken wall and heading left toward the brightly lit room. You'll catch sight of yourself in a mirror. Moving on you'll need to listen closely to the "Door Codes—Dale Little" audio log to learn the security lock code—451—which raises the shutter.

At the bottom of the stairs ahead is "The Machine—Wilson" audio log on a desk that says: "He sees everything." Opening the drawers makes this message even spookier. Check the cabinet beneath the stairs for more mysterious messages after you've done a double take. Keep heading toward the light, which is your only sign of hope, up another tumble-down wall.

When a mystery figure slams a door shut, you'll need to find a switch that activates locker access down the next flight of stairs. That same door is now open. You may now proceed to collect your first upgrade and some slugs from a table next to a locker. With this, you can boost health or stamina—really a choice between running or standing your ground.

Search all the lockers in the vicinity for the maintenance key, a Bendy Bar, and Bacon Soup.

Voice of
WILSON

It seems that Arch Gate Studios, in all its misplaced admiration, was so eager to absorb the life's work of that crooked charlatan, Joey Drew, they didn't fully realize what they had acquired.

Call it fate that I just happened to be there on the loading dock that morning. When the delivery boys dropped one of the crates, it smashed open, and inside there was something truly special.

A mass of yellow steel and beautiful rivets. Some kind of machine. No one knew what it was. So the fools put it on display for all to see. But I could tell that this crude device held secrets. Secrets that could be mine.

New Objective:
UNLOCK MAINTENANCE GATE

The Maintenance gate is across from the lockers, behind a heavy cart. You'll need to push this out of the way. The door that reads, "Caution Keep Closed"? That's right, you'll pull it open. At the end of the corridor, a Striker surprises you at the barred door, then scuttles away. You've reached the Little Devil Lounge, an employee's break room—minus employees.

Voice of
NATHAN ARCH

I'm ready for something different in my career. I've built steel companies from the ground up, dabbled in petroleum, even tried political office once. "That Nathan Arch," they used to say, "he's got the magic touch!" But I'm hungry for a bit of fun, I think. Something both the masses and I can enjoy. My son suggested movies. Open a studio! Now, I love a good film as much as anyone, but the magic of animation, now, there's something special! My old friend Joey knew the thrills of bringing characters to life, rest his soul. Maybe with a bit of elbow grease and a small cash investment, I can resurrect the past.

Directions:

Scour the lounge for any items to scrounge and enjoy a snack if needed. Down the hall, past Butcher Gang standees, you pass through the door to the Animation Department entrance. In front of the ticket booth opposite you'll find the "Inspiration—Nathan Arch" audio log sitting on a crate. Before moving on, head left to an office, where the "The Slug Problem—Hudson Doyle" memo is on the desk, along with lots of slugs for later. Back at the booth, your key breaks in the lock.

New Objective: BREAK THE LOCK

You hear Alice calling you from an old intercom down the hall to the left. She congratulates you on your progress so far, but it sounds like something else just entered the room. Alice urges you to find a Gent pipe ASAP.

FIND THE GENT PIPE

Head back the way you came, away from the intercom, toward the Atrium Supply door. Next to this, through a wire fence, you'll see a creature impaled with the Gent pipe (yuck).

RESTORE POWER TO THE ATRIUM SUPPLY

You'll need to get the lights working before risking the Atrium Supply. But as you start to explore, a mysterious figure crashes into the room, threatening to rip your face off. Nice. He is one of the Lost Ones. Since you are unarmed, you need to wait this one out, using stealth to stay low and out of sight. The Lost One can see and hear any sudden movement.

While the Lost One is busy staring at a desk, sneak through the door that he used to get in. Down here you'll find a break in the wall, the other side of which is a control panel. Perfect! Only . . . the fuse for the Atrium Supply room is blown.

FIND THE FUSE

Stay hidden until the Lost One slinks away, making it possible for you to head back to the Little Devil Lounge. Flee the Striker that springs to attack you along the way, hiding out of sight until it is gone. You'll need to be cautious in the lounge too, as another Lost One is on patrol ("Kitchen's closed!"). Eventually, after much patient hiding, you'll need to sneak into the kitchen behind the counter. In here is the fuse—stuck into a cake like a birthday candle.

New Objective:
FIX THE FUSE BOX

The Lost One is still on the prowl as you make your way back to the broken control panel. His circuit includes investigating the kitchen. This is your chance to sneak away unseen—use the barrel as a hiding spot, which is conveniently placed for this very reason. Now all that's left is to evade the Lost One down Animation Alley and screw the fuse squeakily into place.

GET THE GENT PIPE

You'll need to dodge that Lost One again to reach the Atrium Supply room. Once inside, there's an audio log, "Hiding Treasures—Kay Lee," on a table, guarded by a Bendy plushy. There are lots of Gent parts to collect in here too; don't miss those. Next, head through the break in the wall to reach the room with the Gent pipe-impaled victim. Before approaching that grisly mess, read the "Close Call—Hudson Doyle" memo and grab a Gent battery from the desk. Removing the Gent pipe from the body in the adjoining room raises the stakes quite a bit.

Voice of
KAY LEE

At the end of every crumbling empire, you gotta hide the treasures.

Mister Cohen brought me in to catalog and secure some of Joey Drew's more special assets in places no one will ever find them. Sure, that sounds completely legal, right? Anyway, I'll be leaving some clues around so we can find them later. Just remember, this nonsense wasn't my idea! So, here's my first little hint: I finally found a use for those silly motivational posters here in the atrium offices. They're sure to make quite an impact. I can't believe I just said that.

STUDIO MEMO

CLOSE CALL

We're playing with fire. No question about it. First Gent comes in here and puts thick heavy pipes over everyone's head. Must weigh a ton! Then Joey opens up the place for tours to the general public. Are we really thinking this through? For Pete's sake, Sammy's Music Department is constantly flooded! And while I was giving a tour last week, we almost lost a whole dang wall when a valve blew out! Stupid tour group applauded thinking it was part of the show.

I know Joey is looking to drum up some cash lately. But this, this is just asking for disaster to strike. One good accident and there's going to be a landslide of trouble.

—Hudson Doyle

Directions:

The Gent pipe is your tool for self-defense against the Lost Ones, who fall after a few well-placed bashes. You'll also use the Gent pipe to smash through weak sections of the walls, the first you'll find by heading left out of Atrium Supply. Inside is a small office, where a desk drawer hides the "Strange Money—Grant Cohen" audio log and a filing cabinet holds the memo "Getting Serious—Sally Newt." While you're here: On top of the cabinet is a Gent battery.

Bashing through the next wall takes you to another small office, where the "In My Mind—Unknown" memo is on the desk. If you continue past the standee through the broken wall, this leads to another breakable section that opens out into the Little Devil Lounge.

Voice of
GRANT COHEN

Well, uh, we hit rock bottom. No doubt about it. By all accounts, I don't even know how this studio is still going at all. If you follow the money, you just hit a big old brick wall! Well, let me tell you, blank ledgers, spare cash—you know, weird amounts that plain just don't add up. There's still income finding its way onto the books, but I can only tell you for the life of me, I c-can't figure out where it's all coming from. Though the obvious answer here is that Gent is privately pouring in some funds. And truth be told, they really creep me out. Especially that Mister Gray. He doesn't seem to be motivated by money, and he sure as heck ain't telling us what he's REALLY after. You just can't trust someone like that.

STUDIO MEMO

GETTING SERIOUS

I heard some of the workers from down the hall last night talking about storming Joey Drew's office. They were using some colorful language, banging their fists on the tables and chairs. It was the same bunch who whistled at me yesterday. Things must be getting serious.

That accountant, Grant Cohen, just walks from his desk down to the men's room and back all day. Over and over again, gripping his stomach. Kind of green in the gills. I can't tell if something he ate isn't agreeing with him, or if he just can't take the pressure anymore.

Joey's got a plan, he keeps saying, Gent is making something special. I really hope he's right. I may just be a secretary, but this place has a magic I don't want to see end.

—Sally Newt

THAT **WILSON!** HE'S EVERYWHERE! YET HE'S NOWHERE! I DON'T KNOW HOW HE DOES IT! IT'S **MADNESS! MADNESS!** CAN YOU HEAR ME NOW, WILSON? **CAN YOU?!** YOU WON'T GET ME! I'VE GOT A PLAN! IF I TEAR OUT MY BRAIN, THEN YOU CAN'T HEAR MY MIND! **HA!** I'LL SHOW YOU! I DEFY YOU! ALL HAIL THE **INK DEMON! HAIL!** HE'S NOT DEAD, **I TELL YOU!** HE WILL RISE AGAIN! AND HIS DARK REVENGE WILL BE **TERRIBLE!**

Behind the "Busy Bee" poster in the Getting Serious memo room is a switch. To reveal it, use the Gent pipe. Similar switches are hidden behind a "Trust in Joey" poster in Animation Alley, and the "Take 5" poster in the office where you found the "Slug Problem" memo. When all three are activated, a musical tinkle sounds to tell you that something has changed. The mystery is solved through the Atrium Supply room, through the broken wall that leads to the barred door and beyond that a ladder beneath an Alice Angel standee. In this tiny room you'll find an upgrade, Gent parts, Gent batteries, and a Gent toolkit. You could bash your way out of there through the walls but, sadly, it's a dead end. Figuratively speaking.

New Objective:

BREAK THE LOCK USING THE GENT PIPE

As soon as you've broken in and entered the ticket booth, head straight to the back and flip the wall switch. This opens the shutter on the wall to your right. As you wade through the inky river beyond, you shudder uncontrollably for a while. What was that? Grab your copy of *The Illusion of Living* from the sofa beside a Bendy doll before stepping out of the goo.

A Searcher is clawing at the wall at the end of the next corridor, beneath a daubed message that reads: "You don't have to kill me." True! You now have the power to banish these fiends, but only if you can approach them unawares. The Gent pipe continues to prove its worth as a lock-chopping master key of sorts, opening yet another barred door.

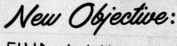

Directions:

In the Animation Alley corridor, to your left when facing the abyss, there is a Card Exchange machine. This asks you to trade Gent items for "One-Time Access" to Safe & Sound Lockers. One such locker has been installed to the right of where you came through the last barred door. There are lots of slugs inside, plus Gent parts and a Gent toolkit.

New Objective:

FIND A WAY TO CROSS THE ABYSS

There's a chasm between you and the elevator up. To overcome this, you'll first need to push a trolley blocking a sliding hatch, which leads to the Employee Locker Room and a power switch. This activates the power for Animation Alley, all lit up as you exit the Locker Room.

Three Lost Ones emerge from behind the door—one female followed by two males. They're tricky to tackle all at once, so lure them into the open, hiding in the Employee Locker Room until you're ready to strike. If you're careful you might even banish one or all three of them.

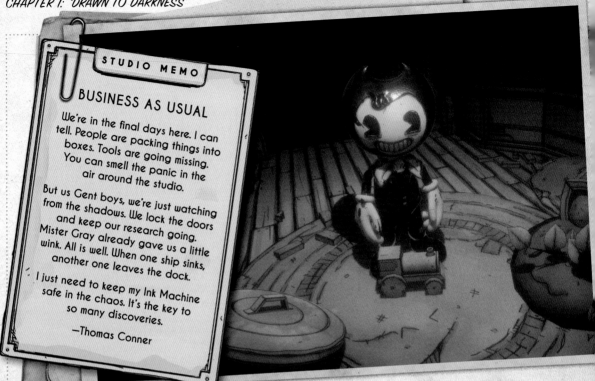

STUDIO MEMO

BUSINESS AS USUAL

We're in the final days here. I can tell. People are packing things into boxes. Tools are going missing. You can smell the panic in the air around the studio.

But us Gent boys, we're just watching from the shadows. We lock the doors and keep our research going. Mister Gray already gave us a little wink. All is well. When one ship sinks, another one leaves the dock.

I just need to keep my Ink Machine safe in the chaos. It's the key to so many discoveries.

—Thomas Conner

Enjoy your studio tour while you're here, learning all about the Writers' Room, Artists' Room, Sound Room, and Editing Room. Then, go back to the entrance where you'll see a vent in the wall beside a barrel. Smash this, and the next one after entering, with the Gent pipe to reach a pokey room. On a stool here you'll find a "Business as Usual—Thomas Conner" memo. The wall switch released the Main Studio security lock, revealing a narrow shaft. To your great surprise, you find Bendy in the room beyond a barred door clutching his toy train. Unfortunately, you almost banish him when he reaches out to touch you, and so he flees . . .

In the next area you see a door that has DON'T KNOCK painted on its portal window. There's also a sign that says NO VISITORS. GO AWAY. So, you stay and you knock. The Lost One who appears at the portal thinks you might be Phil and demands that you bring him his pictures.

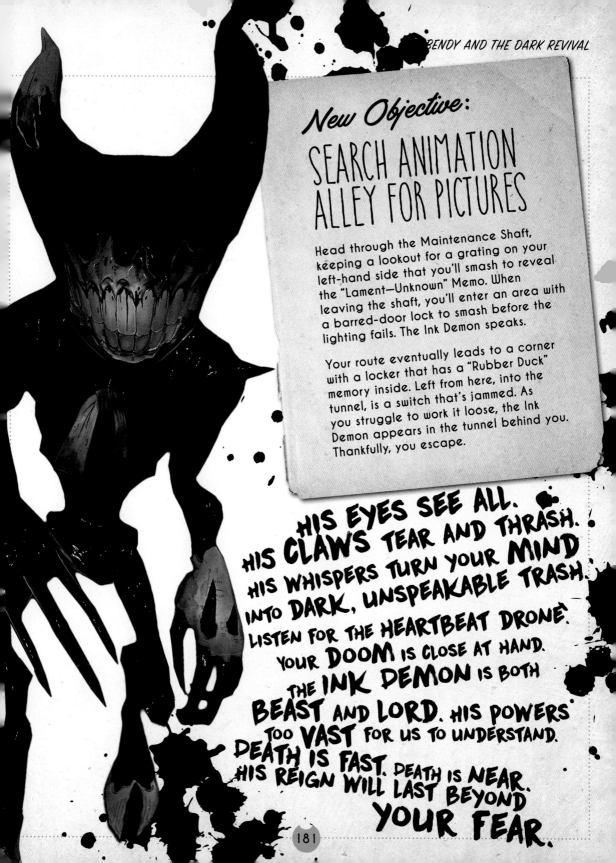

New Objective:

SEARCH ANIMATION ALLEY FOR PICTURES

Head through the Maintenance Shaft, keeping a lookout for a grating on your left-hand side that you'll smash to reveal the "Lament—Unknown" Memo. When leaving the shaft, you'll enter an area with a barred-door lock to smash before the lighting fails. The Ink Demon speaks.

Your route eventually leads to a corner with a locker that has a "Rubber Duck" memory inside. Left from here, into the tunnel, is a switch that's jammed. As you struggle to work it loose, the Ink Demon appears in the tunnel behind you. Thankfully, you escape.

HIS EYES SEE ALL. HIS CLAWS TEAR AND THRASH. HIS WHISPERS TURN YOUR MIND INTO DARK, UNSPEAKABLE TRASH. LISTEN FOR THE HEARTBEAT DRONE. YOUR DOOM IS CLOSE AT HAND. THE INK DEMON IS BOTH BEAST AND LORD. HIS POWERS TOO VAST FOR US TO UNDERSTAND. DEATH IS FAST. HIS REIGN WILL LAST. DEATH IS NEAR. BEYOND YOUR FEAR.

CHAPTER TWO
"THE DEMON'S DOMAIN"

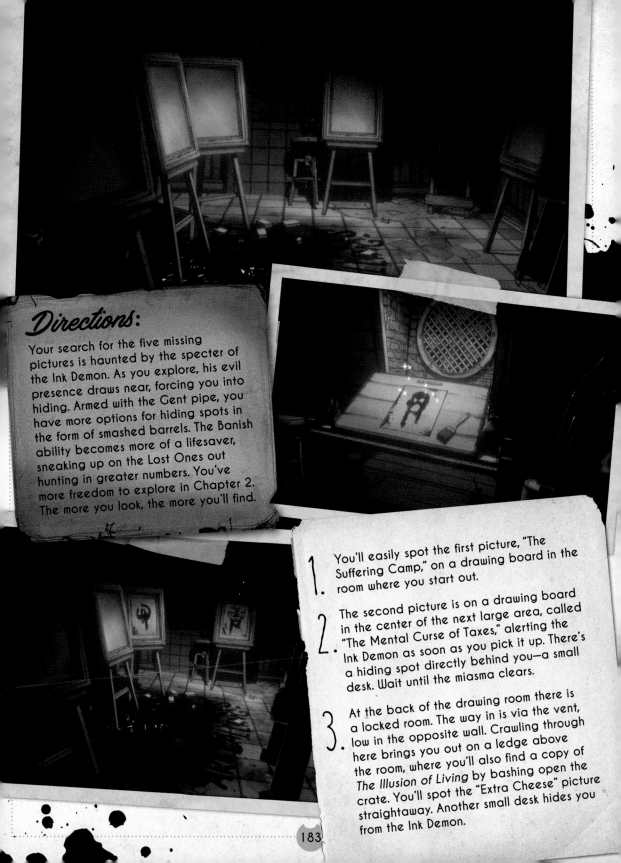

Directions:

Your search for the five missing pictures is haunted by the specter of the Ink Demon. As you explore, his evil presence draws near, forcing you into hiding. Armed with the Gent pipe, you have more options for hiding spots in the form of smashed barrels. The Banish ability becomes more of a lifesaver, sneaking up on the Lost Ones out hunting in greater numbers. You've more freedom to explore in Chapter 2. The more you look, the more you'll find.

1. You'll easily spot the first picture, "The Suffering Camp," on a drawing board in the room where you start out.

2. The second picture is on a drawing board in the center of the next large area, called "The Mental Curse of Taxes," alerting the Ink Demon as soon as you pick it up. There's a hiding spot directly behind you—a small desk. Wait until the miasma clears.

3. At the back of the drawing room there is a locked room. The way in is via the vent, low in the opposite wall. Crawling through here brings you out on a ledge above the room, where you'll also find a copy of The Illusion of Living by bashing open the crate. You'll spot the "Extra Cheese" picture straightaway. Another small desk hides you from the Ink Demon.

Voice of
BILL DANTON

When you animate, it's . . . so much more than just motion.

It's a way of life, an art, a passion. Each tiny movement is an emotional trigger to the audience. Get it wrong, and you will lose them. You must live the characters to draw them. You must feel the motions in your mind. Act them out around your room. Today, I'm a clock, a dancing timekeeper. *Tick tock. Tick tock. Tick tock.* Watch my movements. See my frames of animation! I have so many characters to animate yet. Thousands of frames to go. But for now, I'm just a clock. *Tick tock. Tick tock.*

4. Exit by breaking the lock on a barred door, go through another drawing room, into another vent through which there are two ways to proceed. Following the warm glow leads you into a wide room with a Card Exchange machine. In the adjacent room is a power switch that opens heavy, sliding doors behind you. If, instead, you take the shadowy route, this emerges onto a ledge, dropping you into a room with barrels, a Safe & Sound dispenser containing the audio log "Productive Day—Phil Clark" and "The Bus to Work" picture.

5. Break a barrel to hide when the Ink Demon shows up. The fifth, and final, picture—"Ham Sandwich Agony"—is in the connecting room, accessed via a short, dim-lit tunnel.

Take the next vent out of here, which you'll need to smash through to enter. This leads to the room with the first picture, where you can head down a narrow corridor and activate the "Dancing Clock—Bill Danton" audio log. Behind you is a vent to smash open, taking you back to the drawing room area.

Now return to the easels, passing through the sliding doors, and place the missing pictures. This prompts the Lost One who set the task to sprint out of his hiding place and attack you!

Voice of
PHIL CLARK

This has been the best week of my life

For once, we don't have Mister Drew hanging over our shoulders!

He ain't even stopped by at all. I'm turning out so many frames of animation, I can't even keep up with myself! Now the only thing that's bothering me is that freak two desks over. Recent hire. Real weirdo. He keeps trying to show me some pictures he's been drawing. I tell you, this place has a curse. If it's not one thing stopping you from getting things done, it's another.

Voice of
WILSON

When I first entered this world, it was an untamed wilderness. A wretched, crawling slum, ruled by that grinning Demon. From chaos, I brought order. From order, I brought peace. Once you cut the head from the snake, the snake bleeds out quietly onto the ground. Now the only question that remains is: What if the head grows back?

Directions:

The art-loving Lost One's room leads to the screening rooms and Storyboarding suite. Collect the "Originality—Unknown" memo from the crate before passing through the door.

The Storyboarding suite, to your right, has a projector showing three sketches. Remember them, because you'll need to line these up with the projectors in the screening rooms next door. As you enter the screening rooms, note the hiding place beneath a desk, because as soon as you start snooping, the Ink Demon arrives. You'll find an "Over and Over—Phil Clark" memo on a bench and "The Snake—Wilson" audio log on a table in the main seating area.

You'll need to crawl through a vent at the side of the Projector Booth to find your way inside. Add another edition of *The Illusion of Living* to your collection from the filing cabinet, then match the pictures in order, which gives you the number 235—the security lock passcode. The Ink Demon may pounce the second you've figured this out, so find somewhere to hide!

STUDIO MEMO

OVER AND OVER

You can only watch the same dang cartoon so many times before you go crazy! I'm starting to forget what it was they wanted me to change. Good thing I take notes.

And what's with them little numbers in the corner of the screen? Is that some kind of code? I'd better check with the storyboard room.

—Phil Clark

STUDIO MEMO

ORIGINALITY

Nobody wants to see my pictures! I've worked so hard on them for so long. And they're all my own original work. I'll have to MAKE people look at them. They'll see how talented I am!

But wait, what if someone looks at them and takes all my precious ideas?! NO! THEY CAN'T DO THAT! They're MY original characters! MINE! Do not steal! Do not steal!

Directions:

The sign up ahead reads, "Come Say Hello," so why not do just that? On the table beside a slumped Lost One woman is the audio log "She Is the Fourth—Jane Todd." In this same room is a tall wooden crate that, if opened, unleashes a new terror in the form of Slicer, a disfigured version of Carley—a discarded fourth companion concept for the Butcher Gang. Retrace your steps and pull the security lock switch, which faces the Maintenance door opposite where you'll head next. There's a "Grand Opening—Nathan Arch" audio log as soon as you pass through, before ducking into a broken pipe, then through many corridors.

Voice of
NATHAN ARCH

The papers are signed! The animation staff is hired! Arch Gate Pictures is open for business! As of nine o'clock this morning, Bendy and all his little cartoon friends now belong to me. I'll admit, it's strange owning a dear friend's legacy. But I think Joey would be content knowing it's safely in my hands. "You just gotta believe," he used to say. He was such a showman. Well, I believe Joey. I wholeheartedly believe!

Voice of
JANE TODD

Good things always come in threes, they say. Bendy, Alice, and Boris. It just works. So when I showed my coworkers my design for a new, fourth member of the Butcher Gang, you could almost hear the disgust at the lunch table. "A ghost girl?" they said. "No one's gonna get it." They just laughed at my drawings, crumpled them up like trash. But I'll get Mister Drew on my side. He'll understand. He's got to. Carley will join the Butcher Gang. And she'll be beloved by all. One way or another, I'll bring Carley to life.

A BUTCHERED DECISION ACHIEVEMENT
From the Writers' Room Hallway, follow the "Come Say Hello" sign and open the trunk found in that room. This reveals the Slicer, which randomly attacks throughout the rest of the game. Finish the game under these harrowing conditions to unlock this achievement/trophy.

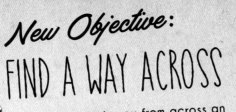

New Objective:
FIND A WAY ACROSS

A Lost One taunts you from across an incomplete walkway. The gap is too wide to jump. This puzzle is swiftly solved, simply requiring the switch to be pulled from a control panel to your right as you face the windows. This lowers a huge pipe, wide enough to run along, that drops into the darkness as soon as you're across. Now your problem is how to make it back!

HELP THE LOST ONE

You'll jog through a large drainage pipe before encountering Porter, the Lost One, who is stuck in a hole—your only way out. Use Banish to loosen him up a little, setting him free.

FOLLOW THE LOST ONE DOWN THE PIPE

At the bottom of the same pipe, Porter names you "Bobby" and, as a gift for helping him out just now, passes on his Flow ability. Flow allows you to access hard-to-reach areas and is a great skill for sneaking at speed. It has a long cooldown time, however, so use it sparingly. Your first attempt is to reach the platform opposite, flowing over a broken wooden floor.

Voice of
LANCE DERBY

Something funny's going on around here. Call me suspicious if you wanna, but I know the signs of weirdness when I see 'em. Don't get me wrong, we've always had visitors around the studio, but lately we're getting just one kind of visitor in particular: Gent Corporation employees. Tons of 'em. They're working in the hallways, ripping up the floors, taking the best toilets, you can't even get near the Little Devil Lounge these days! It's starting to feel less like an animation studio around here, and more and more like some crazy scientist's laboratory.

It's just plain weirdness.

Directions:

Now is the time to explore! After meeting with Porter and acquiring Flow, the new power—along with your trusty Gent pipe—are used to navigate and survive around Animation Alley. Multiple Lost Ones stalk the area, providing practice with Flow and Banish in combination. There's much backtracking to be done elsewhere too.

Returning to the abyss—from "Find a Way Across"— you now have Flow to fly over. A door has opened next to the pipe where you helped Porter, and inside here is an upgrade canister, with which you can now use to improve ability cooldown.

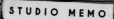

STUDIO MEMO

LOCKER CODE

So get this bit of strangeness: That Thomas Connor guy from the Gent, he's takin' over the back area in the Locker Room. Guess I'll have to move my little office of cardboard boxes somewhere else.

He gave me the code for the door in case I need to ever get in and clean up. I wrote the code down and put it in my locker. It's the eighth locker over from the poster with the pretty lady on it. But I tell ya, if that guy keeps causing trouble for me, I'm outta here!

—Wally Franks

Heading back, past the pictures you'd returned to the Lost One, and through the studio tour, you'll arrive back at the Employee Locker Room. With the Gent pipe you can smash through to the Guys section, where you will find the "Weirdness—Lance Derby" audio log. Grab as much inventory as possible, including a Gent battery and yet another *The Illusion of Living* book. Next to the security lock is a "Locker Code—Wally Franks" memo. It helps you find the code from inside one of the many, many lockers. This code, for future reference, is 215.

New Objective:

GO TO THE GENT UPGRADE STATION

As soon as you've collected the schematic from the crate, your new objective is to upgrade the Gent pipe with the Gent door access mod, which further expands the studio to explore. Simply slot the Gent pipe into the wall-mounted station.

CHARGE YOUR GENT PIPE

Next, you'll need a Gent battery (you'll have plenty by now) to power it up. Deposit this into the charging station next to the upgrade station and turn the handle to juice it up. To exit the room, insert the Gent pipe into the Gent lock. Be sure to charge the pipe before leaving.

STUDIO MEMO

A BIT OF FATE

Fate is a strange thing. Just when you think you've run out of options, it puts a solution in your lap. Andre stopped by my office to say good-bye on his way out the door. As far as everyone else knows, he's gone home to Rio. But he never made it. Never even made it out of the kitchen. Little Andre slumped over dead right in front of me. Barely even made a sound. And here I was worried about running out of meat for today's special. Fate is a strange thing. Just when you think you've run out of options, it puts a solution in your lap.

—Chef Buck

Directions:

Searchers have infested the lockers as you work your way around to Animation Alley, plus a Lost One for good measure. Now that you have the Gent door access mod, backtracking is even more tempting. The kitchen in the Little Devil Lounge has a Gent locked door, the room beyond has the "A Bit of Fate—Chef Buck" memo on a desk next to slugs galore. There's a filing cabinet loaded with Gent batteries too—the kitchen is a treasure trove.

Voice of
SHAWN FLYNN

Well, Shawn! You finally did it! You went and told the boss exactly what's up! "It's time to move on!" I said to him! "This toy man's ready for a new adventure!" I have to admit, he took it far better than I expected. Probably because a lot of other people be ditchin' this month as well. But I don't pay no mind to Mister Drew. I ain't leaving 'cause of that old windbag. No, I've seen far worse in my day. That's for sure! I'm hitting the road 'cause it's time for Shawn Flynn to see some open sky. Find meself a little cabin upstate. Somewhere the family and I can start anew! But before I go, I've made one last toy. A little parting present for the factory lads. Let's see how long it takes them to find it.

STUDIO MEMO

A COMPLAINT

Listen, Angus,

Let me explain a thing or TWO about working on a team. If you expect me to take care of your work while you take FIVE, you're crazy! I even had to lock up the shelf room last night because you had already gone home early. It's your responsibility. Not mine!

I won't be the ONE to take the fall if you do that again, you lazy good for nothing. Next time, I'll let the manager call you out, understand?

Directions:

1. From the lounge, head through the piped corridors to the factory Locker Room.

2. Near the Bendy standee and oil drum, Flow jump through a gap in the fence to a ledge on the far side, to the left. Grab *The Illusion of Living* book, "Moving on—Shawn Flynn" audio log, a Gent battery, and Gent parts.

3. This ledge is near the desk where "He sees everything" is written, from Chapter 1. Banish or bash Lost Ones before finding the message "Where is the Toyman?" above a brightly lit desk.

4. From this room, duck into the tunnel where you'll see a Bendy standee behind a wire fence. Flow over the narrow gap in the fence, into the enclosure to take the Paper Plane memory.

5. From here, head to the Heavenly Toys room. Follow the mezzanine floor, down the stairs to smash barrels for your next *Illusion of Living* book. You should own about twenty now!

6. Back in the Heavenly Toys room, above the short-circuiting wall switch, you can Flow jump up to a security lock. On that same floor is a locker containing the "A Complaint—Unknown" memo.

7. The memo holds the clue for the security lock, emphasizing the numbers two, five, and one. It opens a hatch beyond the barred gate. Flow skillfully around to grab an upgrade canister.

8. Circle all the way back to the Employee Locker Room, and the abyss near Animation Alley. Make sure your Gent pipe is charged at the nearby station. Flow across the gap, activate the Gent lock, and snaffle *The Illusion of Living* book on your way in. The Ink Demon consumes you . . .

TOYMAN'S SECRET ACHIEVEMENT
Find the "Where is the Toyman" message in the Factory Access Entrance area. From here you'll see a Bendy standee behind a wire fence. Flow into this small area and smash the Bendy standee to reveal a small toy robot. Pick this up for the achievement/trophy.

VE DON'T LIVE FOREVER.
HEN WE'RE KILLED OR FINALLY PULLED
APART, OUR DISEASED SOULS RETURN
TO THE INK TO BE **REBORN**. AN
NENDING CYCLE OF **TORMENT**.

BUT SOMETIMES, SOMETHING
EVEN WORSE CAN HAPPEN.
SOUL CAN SLIP FROM THE
NK **COMPLETELY**. IT GETS CAUGHT
BETWEEN WORLDS, UNABLE TO DIE OR RETURN.
THEY WAIL IN THE NIGHT.
RIFTING IN SHADOW. THE PHANTOMS
F THE MACHINE. **THE GHOSTS.**

New Objective:
FIND A NEW WAY TO THE ELEVATORS

Shutters are brought down to bar your route, forcing you back toward the Artist's Rest living quarters. A central office has a button, controlling access to Lost & Found, Sauna Entry, and the Upper Beds.

In one of the alcoves, you'll find lockers for the sauna, one of which contains *The Illusion of Living* book. In the sauna at the back, you'll find "The Ghosts— Unknown" memo. Enter Lost & Found to Flow into a tiny office with the hoist keys and a new schematic. You can now upgrade to the Gent High Impact Mod, allowing you to charge it for heavier impact.

STUDIO MEMO

CRANE KEYS

I put the crane keys in the Lost & Found office. Some dope keeps leaving them out.

—Muncie Dunn

Voice of
NATHAN ARCH

I haven't had much sleep the past few nights. I've been feeling something pulling at my mind. My thoughts fall to the Joey Drew exhibit we opened last week. Outside one or two artists, I don't think I've ever seen a single soul go inside. It's a shame how so many of us refuse to learn from the past—it can give us our greatest lessons. But still, ever since we moved in Joey's old things, there's been a strange feeling around Arch Gate. Like the ghosts of long ago are wandering about. Calling out to me.

Just as you are leaving Lost & Found, the Ink Demon blocks your path, and you beat a hasty retreat to the key room, Flowing to safety until the Ink Demon has gone.

Last, go to the Upper Beds and access the hoist controls. There's a "Crane Keys—Muncie Dunn" memo, telling you where the keys are (you already know: Lost & Found). The crane positions a platform, which you Flow onto from the top of the central office. From the platform you can reach a balcony and collect the Engine Oil memory. At the end of the hall, beneath a message that reads, "Without Fear There Is Chaos" is an upgrade canister.

You want to be heading for the exit, however, which is back across the platform and onto another ledge. Collect "The Exhibit—Nathan Arch" audio log, triggering Chapter 3.

CHAPTER THREE
"THE ETERNAL MACHINE"

Directions:

Your growing powers and capabilities help to battle tougher foes and perform greater acts of agility in Chapter 3. In "The Eternal Machine," your skills are becoming second nature.

Shortly after picking up the last audio log ("The Exhibit—Nathan Arch") you'll pass a Gent Upgrade Station—using one of your Gent batteries—on the way to a Gent Charging Station.

STUDIO MEMO

TRAFFIC JAM

We're in and out like rats! Scurrying all over the place. People shoving and pushing. The way the elevator system is set up you'd think we had only ten employees working here. At any time of the day, this hall is full of people waiting to go up. Right around quitting time, you're going to have to grab a magazine and wait your turn. It just goes to show that Joey Drew Studios really did grow too much too fast.

But I hear there's more than one way to escape this rat's maze. I'm going to do some asking around.

—Hudson Doyle

Take your fully charged Gent pipe back to the Upgrade Station to acquire the shock pipe, after bashing the Lost One that gets in your way. You'll next need to activate the Gent locked door just up ahead. Remember to recharge before passing through. To the left, next to the studio tour speaker, is a locker where you'll find a copy of *The Illusion of Living*.

Follow the corridor around to the elevator lobby, where the "Traffic Jam—Hudson Doyle" memo is resting on one of the benches. As you explore the seating areas farther along, breaking padlocks and sliding a cart out of the way as you go, you'll find a room with lots of lockers and a Safe & Sound dispenser behind a Gent locked door. A Card Exchange machine is just next door—if you are not already equipped.

Directions:

As you head down toward the elevators, the Ink Devil is there waiting, forcing you to hide. There's a Little Miracle Station at the top of the stairs, to your right, in case you missed it. Once the coast is clear, head back to the elevator. Before you step inside, smash the wall to the left where you'll find the "Who We Are—Unknown" memo.

WE LIVE IN THE **RUINS OF THE PAST**. FOREVER LOST IN THE SHADOWS OF THOSE WHO CAME BEFORE US. **BLENDED SOULS** TO MAKE SOMETHING NEW. **BIRTHED FROM A MACHINE** INTO A WORLD WE CANNOT OWN. BUT THE **INK DEMON LIVES IN ALL OF US**. A VOICE THAT CALLS US TO A PURPOSE. WE KNOW IT'S A LIE, BUT HIS **INTOXICATING** PULL IS STRONG. HE IS CALLING. ALWAYS **CALLING. CAN YOU** NOT HEAR HIM?

New Objective: WIDOW KING BOSS BATTLE

All seems fine in the elevator until it grinds to a sudden halt, and a ragged Keeper's voice announces, "Unauthorized surface elevator in use. Manual lift ejection activated." It doesn't sound good, and it isn't. The floor gives way, and you plummet to the Widow King's lair.

As tiny widows snap at your heels, the best course of action is to whack four switches shut, which are mounted on the metal pillars. They require a few hits with the Gent pipe to close. There's no point battling the smaller widows because they just keep coming; stay alive by guzzling coffee from the dispenser at fifteen slugs per shot! Charge your shock pipe at the wall.

Once the switches are all done, the Widow King emerges from the center of the floor to chase you. He backs off after four or five hits with the pipe, sending his minions after you while he recovers. Now you can whack them, refueling on coffee, recharging the shock pipe as you go. You should have enough slugs, but there's a barrel of them in here if needed.

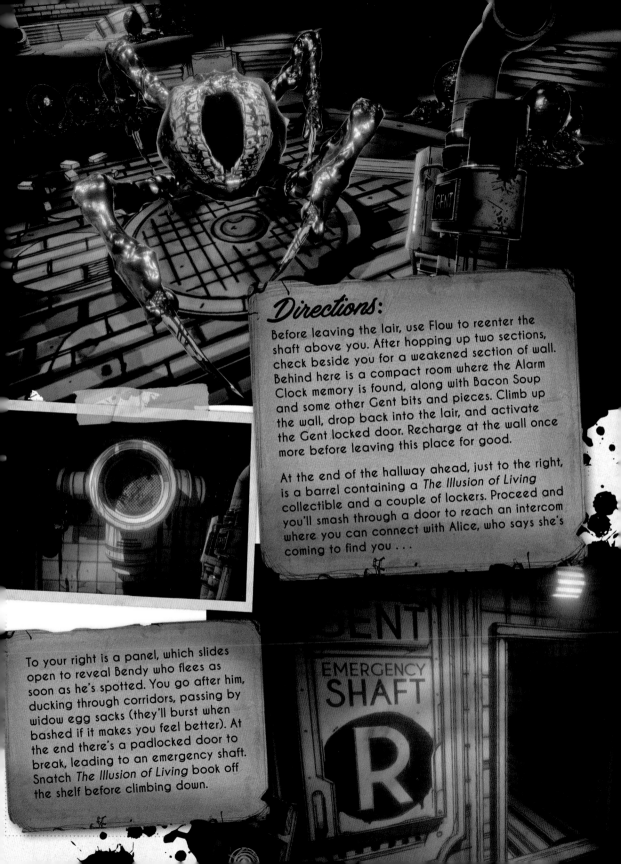

Directions:

Before leaving the lair, use Flow to reenter the shaft above you. After hopping up two sections, check beside you for a weakened section of wall. Behind here is a compact room where the Alarm Clock memory is found, along with Bacon Soup and some other Gent bits and pieces. Climb up the wall, drop back into the lair, and activate the Gent locked door. Recharge at the wall once more before leaving this place for good.

At the end of the hallway ahead, just to the right, is a barrel containing a *The Illusion of Living* collectible and a couple of lockers. Proceed and you'll smash through a door to reach an intercom where you can connect with Alice, who says she's coming to find you . . .

To your right is a panel, which slides open to reveal Bendy who flees as soon as he's spotted. You go after him, ducking through corridors, passing by widow egg sacks (they'll burst when bashed if it makes you feel better). At the end there's a padlocked door to break, leading to an emergency shaft. Snatch *The Illusion of Living* book off the shelf before climbing down.

Directions:

Here you'll meet Joey Drew "in the flesh" . . . so to speak, who explains a little about the realm in which you are trapped—"an ink-stained nightmare." He warns about the Keepers, directing you toward the old Gent Workshop, beyond the sewers, for answers. You have a chance to explore his cramped living space before saying farewell at this point, retrieving the "Something Familiar—Your Best Pal" memo from the bed, and other bits from a trunk. On the bookshelf above the bed is yet another copy of *The Illusion of Living* book.

STUDIO MEMO

SOMETHING FAMILIAR

Every great story begins in mystery. Although things may be dark at the start, the truth will illuminate your way. Don't be afraid of who you are. Fear only what you may become, and banish it away.

—Your Best Pal

STUDIO MEMO

WHITE RABBIT

Don't ever lose hope. When in doubt, the answer you seek is usually nearby. We all have dreams, ghosts in our past. But those ghosts can give us the path forward.

—Your Best Pal

As you exit, turn left past what appears to be Joey's tombstone, toward a room where the memo "White Rabbit—Your Best Pal" can be collected, along with a few Gent parts. As you proceed through the emergency shaft, you'll see Bendy, who makes another swift getaway. Turn right to rummage through a Gent container and go to the end of the section to listen to a "Dark Places—Grace Conway" audio log. Recharge the Gent pipe on the side opposite.

Voice of

GRACE CONWAY

I'm a fan of darkness. It just appeals to me. As old Norman would often say, people really become themselves when they're hidden in shadow. That creepy guy always had a story to tell about this place. But I think I've found a few narrow passages even he didn't know about. I can watch. I can listen. I can even steal. And no one ever sees me. I'm just a ghost, living in the walls, peering from the darkness.

Voice of
JACK FAIN

You gotta follow your inspirations when you're a musician. Stick to what you know works. But when they built the new studio buildings, they all but filled in my office down in the old sewers. Turns out, I've gotten so accustomed to working in those disgusting conditions, that now if my office doesn't stink, the lyrics I write do. So when Gent started digging its massive utility shaft between its place and ours, I knew it would be just the right spot for me to move in. Now, I've got a song in my heart and a creative stench up my nose.

STUDIO MEMO

TUNNEL CONTROLS

They designed this big tunnel to link their new Gent building to Joey Drew Studios. They want to keep labor and parts flowing between them. I don't think they fully knew what they was actually creating here.

When workers are heading through the shaft, you gotta drain the center duct into the overflow. When they're gone, you flood it again. Any schmuck can do it, even if they're not an engineer. But the main thing is, you gotta make sure all the duct hatches are all open! Once they're open, the overflow can go drain back and forth between the two ducts.

Simple stuff, but a bit complicated when you're working by yourself.

—Muncie Dunn

After activating the control panel, climb down the ladder into the pit and turn left under the arches, to the Unsafe Area. Tracking left along the gantry above, there are lockers ahead of another room, which—other than Bacon Soup—seems to hold nothing of interest. However, behind the Barley standee is a small room that has the "Sewer Songs—Jack Fain" audio log. Flip the "Security Override" switch while you're here, then head to the opposite side of the gantry. Here, the rooms lead to a security lock, lined with lockers and holding an upgrade capsule. At this stage you ought to have activated six out of nine upgrade capsules, which suit your style of approach.

As you work your way around, before powering up the Gent locked door out of here, head left to the end of the passage to collect the "Tunnel Controls—Muncie Dunn" memo next to a locker hiding spot. Behind the Gent locked door is a large security override panel, giving you access to the "Emergency Overflow" switch, found behind the large hiding-place locker.

Directions:

Pressing the "Emergency Overflow" switch lowers the ink level, to the point where you can drop into the pit and lift the cover from one of the drainage pipes. You'll then head back to the "Emergency Overflow" switch to raise the ink levels back up again. This attracts three Lost Ones, best handled by hiding in the Little Miracle Station across from the Emergency Overflow console, and then Banishing them one by one. Failing this, constrict them to a corridor for easier bashing.

New Objective:

LORD AMOK

After dealing with these—taking note of their elaborate "hair" styles—Flow jump to the back of the room where the boxes are on a wooden ledge next to a platform with a control panel. More Lost Ones rush your position; Banished in a similar way as before, only this time hide in a locker facing the control panel. After using the Emergency Overflow one last time, follow the walkway all the way around to the right—beating up the final Lost One straggler—and jump down into the pit, heading toward the low-lit room that is now open with the "Next in Line—Unknown" memo inside. A Gent Recharge Station is in the area above and to the left. Above and to the right is where you need to head next. A switch opens a panel, leading to the Throne Room of the Amok leader. Without hesitation, he orders four followers to attack. After vanquishing them with your formidable shock pipe blows and skillful maneuvering, Lord Amok joins the fray. Defeating him results in you becoming the new Amok!

WITHIN OUR ISOLATED WALLS, LORD AMOK REIGNS.

THE DRIPS AND DROPS OF THE LEAKING WORLD ABOVE CANNOT STOP HIS RULE.

THOSE WHO OPPOSE AMOK'S HAND HAVE THEIR BODIES CRUSHED AND FED INTO THE NARROW PIPES THAT LEAD BELOW INTO FORGOTTEN SEWERS UNDER OUR FEET.

THOSE TUNNELS ARE EVEN DEEPER, EVEN DARKER, THAN THIS ONE. THERE IS ONLY SUFFERING DOWN THERE.

BUT, SHOULD ANYONE DEFEAT LORD AMOK, CAST HIM DOWN OUR SMALL KINGDOM WILL BELONG TO THE CONQUEROR.

THIS IS THE SECRET OF AMOK'S IMMORTALITY. PASS ON THE THRONE, PASS ON THE NAME.

Your exalted position grants you access to the "treasure" room, behind the scruffy podium, where slugs and Gent items are yours to claim from the table. Empty their lockers too.

Across from the treasure room there is a Gent Emergency Shaft control panel. Throwing this switch opens the route to the sewers behind the wall that faces the throne-room podium.

The Ink Demon suggests very strongly, "You will accept your fate," as you continue on . . .

CHAPTER FOUR
"FACTORY OF HORRORS"

New Objective:

LOCATE THE GENT BUILDING

As you make your way to the end of the road, search an old car for the "Trouble Town—Kitty Thompson" audio log. Other items can be scrounged from trash cans and mailboxes. Upon reaching the Unsafe Area—across from Good Tower Café—you realize that you need an ID card to pass through.

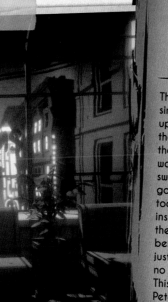

Voice of
KITTY THOMPSON

This old town really has changed ever since that big Gent Building went up. Yesterday, I took a trip over to the Farmer's Market, and they had the whole dang street ripped up! It was like a large hole had just plain swallowed the sidewalk. Men were going in and out with strange iron tools. Kind of looked like they were installing some kind of tunnel under the road. Pipes just everywhere! Pete behind the produce counter was just shaking his head. "They're up to no good," he kept sayin'. "You'll see. This is how it always starts." I think old Pete might be right. But I don't like to dismiss people just on rumors. Only time will tell, I suppose.

New Objective:
FIND AN ID CARD

Eventually, with help from Bendy, you'll find the "Daily Headache—Eugene Lloyd" memo in a trash can near the station. This points to a room in the Downside Hotel. By chance, a Lost One is being thrown out onto the street from a nearby butcher's shop (Grand Chops: Choice Meatly Products). The shop provides a shortcut to an alley leading to the hotel, but you'll need to dispatch the Lost One in the street first, and there's another one loitering in the alley.

Before entering the hotel, search a nearby bench for the "New Job—Steve McGregor" audio log. Across from the Downside Hotel is a boarded-up building. Wonder if anyone is home?

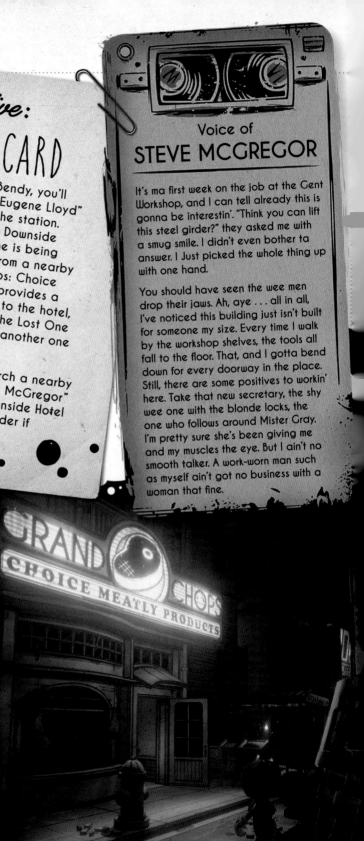

Voice of
STEVE McGREGOR

It's ma first week on the job at the Gent Workshop, and I can tell already this is gonna be interestin'. "Think you can lift this steel girder?" they asked me with a smug smile. I didn't even bother ta answer. I just picked the whole thing up with one hand.

You should have seen the wee men drop their jaws. Ah, aye . . . all in all, I've noticed this building just isn't built for someone my size. Every time I walk by the workshop shelves, the tools all fall to the floor. That, and I gotta bend down for every doorway in the place. Still, there are some positives to workin' here. Take that new secretary, the shy wee one with the blonde locks, the one who follows around Mister Gray. I'm pretty sure she's been giving me and my muscles the eye. But I ain't no smooth talker. A work-worn man such as myself ain't got no business with a woman that fine.

STUDIO MEMO

DAILY HEADACHE

The future has arrived. I just didn't know it would get here so soon. Some of the stuff that's coming out of Gent doesn't follow any of the rules of physics that I know. Hard to believe they started out as a bricklaying company once upon a time.

Nowadays, we have all the modern conveniences and, worse yet, the headaches. Take that ID card machine they've got at the door. You don't bring your ID, you ain't gettin' to work. So I started putting my ID card on my nightstand in my room at the Downside Hotel.

It's not the safest place, but at least I know where it is.

—Eugene Lloyd

Once inside the hotel you'll find that the elevator is out of service, but you can Flow up through the broken floors. On the third floor, use a Gent card on the Safe & Sound locker to collect Joey Drew's *The Illusion of Living* book. You spy the ID card on a bedside table, but as you reach to take it, Drew himself appears, seemingly from out of nowhere.

To help you understand more about what is happening, Drew sends your mind to the Joey Drew Studios Production Room, where a version of himself invites you to take a seat. Before accepting his offer, make sure to look around. A copy of *The Illusion of Living* is under a drawing table.

Flowing through a hole in the ceiling takes you to a room with the "Chapter One—Wally Franks" audio log in a drawer. Dropping down, you find an old desk with early sketches of Bendy. A shutter opens to bring you back into the room with Drew. Across the way—heading right from where you came in—you'll see the message "Dreams Come True" daubed on the wall. Above the connecting corridor, among the rafters, you'll find a "Box of Crayons" memory.

Now return to Drew, who has quite the revelation to make . . .

MOON SHIVER

While exploring the city and searching for the ID card to gain access to the Gent Building, find and smash ten tiny pots. After the last one lies broken, look to the sky. It's not for the fainthearted, but you simply must stop and stare. The event ends as soon as you turn away.

IT STINKS ACHIEVEMENT

Bendy points to an otherwise unassuming door, which prompts you to knock. Rap five times and you'll hear a man complaining about there being too many bad movies that never end.

Voice of
WALLY FRANKS

At this point, I don't get what Joey's plan is for this company. The animations sure aren't being finished on time anymore. And I certainly don't see why we need this . . . machine. It's noisy, it's messy. And who needs that much ink anyway?

Also, get this: Joey had each one of us "donate" something from our workstations. We put them on these little pedestals in the break room. "To help appease the gods," Joey says. "Keep things going."

I think he's lost his mind, but hey, he writes the checks.

But I tell you what, if one more of these pipes burst, I'm outta here.

New Objective:
MAKE YOUR WAY TO THE GENT BUILDING

Armed with the uncomfortable truth of your existence, you work your way back to the Unsafe Area, through the Butcher shop, and where the streets are plagued by Lost Ones. Before using the ID card, pop into the Good Tower Café, now open, to use the upgrade canister.

New Objective:
ENTER THE GENT BUILDING

After passing through the Unsafe Area, you first greet the Ink Demon who, inexplicably, sheds his skin to reveal Bendy . . . who quietly exits the scene. Quite a shock! You continue on through the double doors ahead, straightaway finding the "Paid to Die—Archie Carter" audio log. Farther along, behind the reception desk, is a bookshelf with *The Illusion of Living* to pick up. In the connecting corridor is a Gent Upgrade Station. Through a barred window you'll also see a whiteboard with "523" on it, which is for the next security lock.

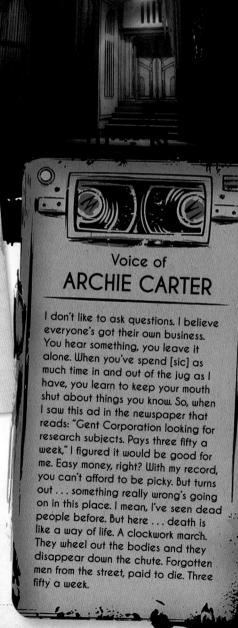

Voice of
ARCHIE CARTER

I don't like to ask questions. I believe everyone's got their own business. You hear something, you leave it alone. When you've spend [sic] as much time in and out of the jug as I have, you learn to keep your mouth shut about things you know. So, when I saw this ad in the newspaper that reads: "Gent Corporation looking for research subjects. Pays three fifty a week," I figured it would be good for me. Easy money, right? With my record, you can't afford to be picky. But turns out . . . something really wrong's going on in this place. I mean, I've seen dead people before. But here . . . death is like a way of life. A clockwork march. They wheel out the bodies and they disappear down the chute. Forgotten men from the street, paid to die. Three fifty a week.

Directions:

A brief, hostile rendezvous with the Keepers forces you into the vents to escape poison gas. The vents wind toward the workshop areas, where you will encounter more deadly Keepers. From the first room—with a curious cloth-covered table—go upstairs to the Gent Charging Station. On the ground floor, at the back of the room behind the patrolling Keeper, is a low section leading to a room with the "Keeper Log 13" audio log on a table next to slugs and a typewriter. The wall switch opens a passage to your left as you exit this room.

You'll reach a room with huge containers and a Keeper. Up the ladder, to your right before the Dishy Cantina, you'll find a kitchen area with the "Keeper Log 26" audio log on a counter. At the back of the room, looking left of the stairs leading to the Condemned Area, is a platform stacked with boxes. Use Flow to hop up there and find the "True Daughter—Joey" memo.

Voice of
KEEPER LOG 13

Experiment thirteen: The Ink Demon is successfully sedated for transport. Laboratory 9 is prepared for arrival at the receiving bay. Be advised that sedation will not last long. Termination must commence immediately upon reception. Wilson will expect a detailed report of the creature's demise.

Voice of
KEEPER LOG 26

Experiment twenty-six: Frequent delays due to the Ink Demon's refusal to terminate. Keepers have administered quarter hourly sessions of physical tortures and surgical invasions to wear down his powers. All of these efforts have been ultimately unsuccessful. A new method of control must be devised. Termination impossible.

STUDIO MEMO

TRUE DAUGHTER

Who would have ever dreamed? In the declining years of my life, I have someone more precious to me than any piece of art I could make. For all the evil that's come from me, this is something finally good. When she laughs and smiles, it fills my heart so much it overflows.

We play and talk as we both learn from each other. There's not much time so every moment has to count. Unlike my versions that came before her, the ones who called me their "uncle," I'm proud to have her call me "Dad." Because she is truly my daughter.

—Joey

Directions:

Heading left from the entrance, up into the passageway, you'll reach another Unsafe Area ("Please have your identification ready") where an enormous Lurker is blocking the way. Above the Lurker, up a ladder, you'll find the "Feeding Time—Unknown" memo on an oil drum and the "Keeper Log 44" audio log near some books on a table toward the back. Don't miss the upgrade capsule on the bench opposite, which brings your total to eight.

Return to the container room with the Keeper and cautiously approach the "Condemned" section at the back, up the stairs. After entering the room and short-circuiting the switch to the Cycle Breakers' containment area, a young female Lost One strikes up a conversation. She wants to play hide-and-seek. If you find her, she'll let you through to the door.

Voice of
KEEPER LOG 44

Experiment forty-four: We have successfully pressed the Ink Demon into the form designated as Bendy. He is smaller in size and harmless in this more timid state. His powers are also greatly reduced. Using lengths of steel wire to cut into the side of his body, he now registers emotional responses. There were tears of ink documented. Screams of pain. It was delightful to see such progress. The Ink Demon will remain in this small form indefinitely.

New Objective:
SEEK OUT HEIDI

Heidi is not too hot at hide-and-seek. She is quite easily found, crouching in the corridor leading to the Lurker, nestled between boxes and a steel drum. She gives you "something special"—the Fast Travel ability—and opens the Cycle Breakers' door as promised. Fast Travel opens linker pipes to surf between specific locations, making backtracking easier.

THE KEEPERS HAVE TAKEN **MY FRIEND!** LOCKED HIM AWAY LIKE SOME ANIMAL! JUST 'CAUSE HE'S BIG AND STRONG.

BUT THEY DON'T NEED TO FEAR HIM! **NO!** IF THEY JUST MAKE SURE TO FEED HIM ON TIME, **BIG STEVE WON'T EVER HURT A FLY!**

HE **LOVES** THE FOOD FROM THE LITTLE DEVIL LOUNGE BEST. IF ONLY SOMEONE WOULD TAKE THE LONG ROAD BACK THROUGH THE SEWERS, CLIMB UP THE **ELEVATOR SHAFT**, AND SEEK OUT HIS FAVORITE THUMPING **DELICACY**. THEN THEY WOULD SEE HOW HARMLESS HE REALLY IS!

Directions:

With the Cycle Breaker section now open, you'll pass through a decontamination zone to access the holding cells. You may recognize Subject 414. This "Mysterious Man" tells a story with details you'll do well to remember. His cell is in a dark corner at the back of the area. Pull the switch to learn more about the Cycle, the Ink Demon, and a particular roll of film.

On the upper level, accessed via Flow or by climbing the ladder, you'll see a table with a "Contraband" sign hanging over it. Just to the right of this is a pile of boxes where you can collect another *The Illusion of Living* book. Across the way is the "Security Lock" switch needed to enter Research—aka "The Pit." Before pressing the Entry button to The Pit, search the darkened section of the room, to your left, for the "Milk Carton" memory.

Press the button if you dare. Wilson needs your help . . .

THE LURKER

You can use linker pipes to backtrack all the way to Animation Alley, via the subway station where you befriended Bendy, and through the lair of the Widow King. You're heading to the Little Devil Lounge, and the kitchen behind the counter, where an Ink Heart is being fried in a pan on the stove beside the fridge-freezer. There are many Lost Ones out to find you, and the Ink Demon is back on the prowl. Your combat and evasion skills are pretty high level at this point.

Retrace your steps—ideally via the linker pipes—to the Lurker and hand over the Ink Heart. Satisfied, the Lurker moves aside and settles down to his favorite snack, like eating an apple. Use the wall switch to open the door, leading to a room stacked with items that handily include a Gent card to open the Safe & Sound locker. The most important item in the Safe & Sound locker is a schematic, which allows you to upgrade the Gent pipe.

Remember there is a Gent Upgrade Station behind the reception desk of the Gent Building, near security lock no. 523. With this you can unlock the Gent Coil Stun Mod—double charging the Gent pipe to stun Keepers on impact, disorienting them "for a fast getaway."

CHAPTER FIVE
"THE DARK REVIVAL"

SECRETS OF THE SUBWAY

Hop off the subway platform at Track 77 (where you'll find Kitty Thompson's "Ghost Train" memo) and walk down the tracks. You'll see a giant paper bird behind bars, pecking at a message from Joey Drew that reads, "Just a Pencil and a Dream." Return to Track 77 at 4:14 (a.m. or p.m.), and you'll witness the spooky phenomenon that Kitty mentions in her writing.

Directions:

Once again, you are in conversation with Wilson, who you can only trust so far, but going along for the ride—literally, on a train. As you consider his words, the train draws to a halt, which is your cue to grab a Gent pipe from the carriage farther down. You'll pass a Keeper as you accompany Wilson off the train, all disconcerting, but that's been your entire day.

Before tagging along with Wilson to his Retreat, take time to explore the station, walking straight ahead through the door. A padlocked gate leads to a platform where you'll find the "Ghost Train—Kitty Thompson" memo on the bench, under a spotlight.

STUDIO MEMO

GHOST TRAIN

Old Track 77 is a quiet place these days.

Ever since that terrible crash a few years back, people don't like to hang around. Too many strange things keep happening on this platform. Last week, one of the railmen told me they had had reports of some train going through that wasn't on the schedule. There were figures standing in the cars, staring through the windows. But it never stopped to let no one off. Just kept on going straight through.

Some say it was the Silverlane Express. The train that crashed.

—Kitty Thompson

Back on the trail of Wilson, beyond a Lost One being roughed up by a Keeper, break through the padlocked gate to your right where the lockers hide a copy of *The Illusion of Living*. As you rejoin Wilson at the top of the stairs, the Ink Demon warns you not to trust him. You keep this to yourself as Wilson opens the checkpoint door.

Wilson is also vigilant—you're required to be security scanned by a Keeper, exposing your Gent pipe as a weapon. Leave this on the counter behind you, next to the Tommy gun and axe, to clear the security check. Wilson then explains about his Security Towers, which nullify your powers and keep the Ink Demon at bay. You then meet Betty, Wilson's kind housekeeper. Betty shows you to your room in the South Wing.

CHECKPOINT

WEAPONS ARE NOT ALLOWED BEYOND THIS POINT. PLEASE PLACE ALL WEAPONS AND CONTAINED INK ON THE HOLDING DESK TO THE RIGHT.

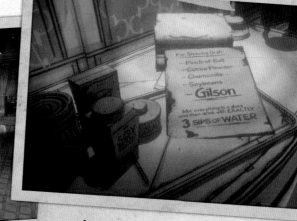

Voice of
WILSON

The machine speaks to me revealing its [sic] many possibilities. What I can accomplish using its power is beyond any measure. Life and death can become a thing of the past. Poverty and hunger, a distant memory. I can remake the world anew. But does the world deserve such a gift? For now, I have bigger matters at hand. A man in a black coat came asking at the front desk about the machine. Said he was from the Gent Corporation. Fortunately, the receptionist knew nothing and he left quietly. Later, I found his name on the sign-in form. Mister Alan Gray.

New Objective:
FIND A GILSON

After you take a brief look around, playing the gramophone and reading a few passages from *The Mug and the Maiden,* which is left on the pillow, Betty offers you her sleep remedy. The ingredients are on a small table, but something is missing: a "Gilson." As you step out of the room, take a left where you'll find the "A Gift to Mankind—Wilson" audio log on the chaise longue.

Back along the hall and to your right is the library, where there are several books to read, but the one of most interest is *Fisherman Jeb's Fish Guide,* which reveals what a Gilson is. Before leaving, collect a copy of *The Illusion of Living,* tucked in the left corner bookshelf.

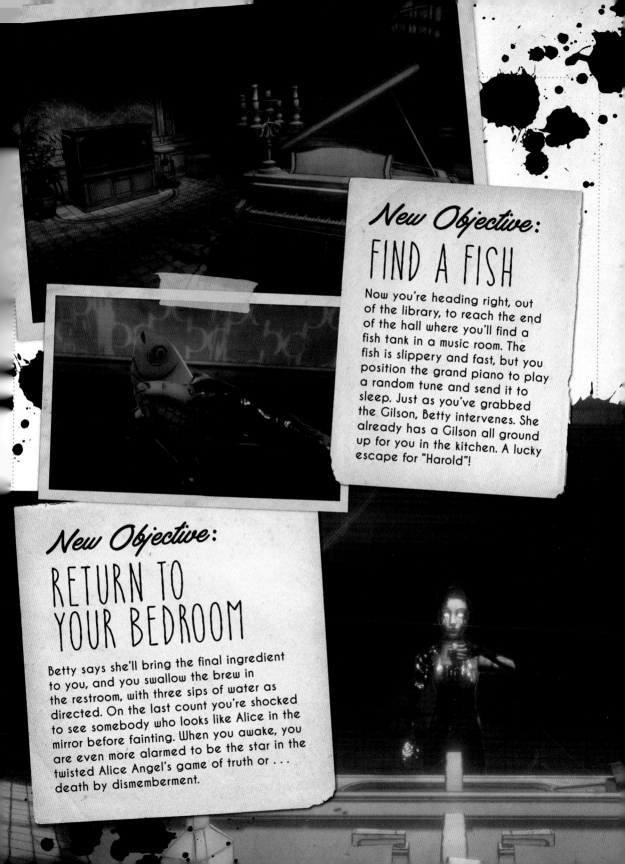

New Objective:
FIND A FISH

Now you're heading right, out of the library, to reach the end of the hall where you'll find a fish tank in a music room. The fish is slippery and fast, but you position the grand piano to play a random tune and send it to sleep. Just as you've grabbed the Gilson, Betty intervenes. She already has a Gilson all ground up for you in the kitchen. A lucky escape for "Harold"!

New Objective:
RETURN TO YOUR BEDROOM

Betty says she'll bring the final ingredient to you, and you swallow the brew in the restroom, with three sips of water as directed. On the last count you're shocked to see somebody who looks like Alice in the mirror before fainting. When you awake, you are even more alarmed to be the star in the twisted Alice Angel's game of truth or . . . death by dismemberment.

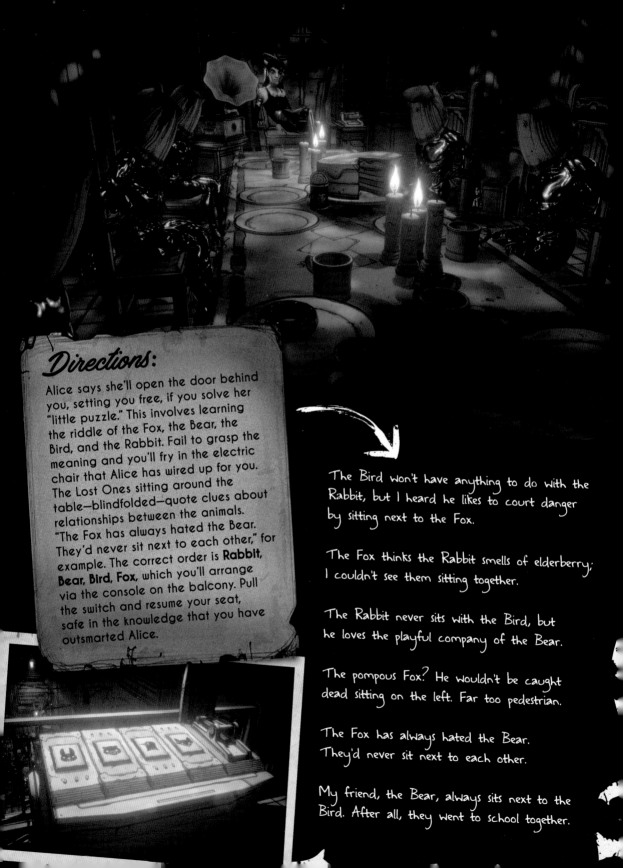

Directions:

Alice says she'll open the door behind you, setting you free, if you solve her "little puzzle." This involves learning the riddle of the Fox, the Bear, the Bird, and the Rabbit. Fail to grasp the meaning and you'll fry in the electric chair that Alice has wired up for you. The Lost Ones sitting around the table—blindfolded—quote clues about relationships between the animals. "The Fox has always hated the Bear. They'd never sit next to each other," for example. The correct order is **Rabbit, Bear, Bird, Fox**, which you'll arrange via the console on the balcony. Pull the switch and resume your seat, safe in the knowledge that you have outsmarted Alice.

The Bird won't have anything to do with the Rabbit, but I heard he likes to court danger by sitting next to the Fox.

The Fox thinks the Rabbit smells of elderberry; I couldn't see them sitting together.

The Rabbit never sits with the Bird, but he loves the playful company of the Bear.

The pompous Fox? He wouldn't be caught dead sitting on the left. Far too pedestrian.

The Fox has always hated the Bear. They'd never sit next to each other.

My friend, the Bear, always sits next to the Bird. After all, they went to school together.

Directions:

After you escape from Alice, you'll retrieve the Gent pipe from a table facing two vending machines and a Gent Charging Station. You'll need the pipe to fend off furious Lost Ones and vending machine snacks to recover any lost health in the attack. Recharge the Gent pipe to deactivate the Security Tower, then charge again in preparation for what lies ahead.

Your way out is up a ladder, across from the Security Tower. Following the corridor leads you to a ledge from where you'll Flow to the balcony opposite. As you approach a brick wall festooned with Alice Angel banners, it shatters under Tommy gun fire from an enraged Alice.

A ladder leads up to a Gent locked door, which your charged Gent pipe powers through. Inside you'll find a console—pull the switch. The weakened wall to the left of the console hides an upgrade capsule, the last you'll need! Grab the Gent battery while you're here.

You'll be heading left, back down the ladder, across the floor space in front of Alice and her hail of bullets—over to where Alice shot down some boxes. Hug the walls, use Flow to avoid being peppered, and cross to a room with a Gent Charging Station (breaking the lock to enter). Along the way, scan the shelves near the darkened wall for a copy of *The Illusion of Living*.

Next, you'll Flow up into the space above the fallen boxes to activate a second Gent locked door. Here you'll flip the switch on another control panel, and jog back out to face Alice. She machine-guns more boxes, revealing a route you'll use to sneak up on her while she taunts.

New Objective:
BANISH ALICE ANGEL

Use Flow to reach the floor above the fallen boxes, this time circling around behind Alice. Though the instruction is to Banish her, this action fails, both you and Alice taking a heavy fall. Alice recovers first and is ready to riddle you full of holes this time, but Alice—the other, friendly, attractive Alice—saves your life just in time. Nice Alice, who you rename Allison, introduces you to Tom, her "protector" (the wolf Alice mentioned). Tom likes being petted.

STUDIO MEMO

STOLEN BEAUTY

Beautiful people run this world. If you can have brains or talent, you may just sneak through the gates. But with a pretty face, every door opens. The crowds bow to you. They ask your name. They want you to attend. They ask you to speak. A silky voice with gorgeous lips is everyone's weak spot.

I was reborn with my perfection stolen from me. To get it back, I'll rip this rotted world apart. Angels are beautiful. Angels are beautiful.

—Alice Angel

Directions:

Now turn to explore the corridor behind you, away from Alice and Tom, to retrieve the "Stolen Beauty—Alice Angel" memo. You'll need to crouch a few times to reach the next area, which is patrolled by a highly attentive Keeper. To make matters worse, Security Towers have disabled your powers, which means no Flow or Banish for a while. You can play cat and mouse, using hiding spots to approach the Lost One's body dropped by the Keeper.

You'll need to use the cabinet hiding spot in the far corridor to sneak past the Keeper and continue your journey. Quickly charge your Gent pipe at the Gent Charging Station, then flip the nearby wall switch to enter the room where you'll find the "Two of a Kind—a Friend" memo on a barrel near the wall immediately to your left. At the back of this same room, you'll also find a music box that could be useful as a distraction . . . only it's broken.

STUDIO MEMO

TWO OF A KIND

Dear Alice,

I don't know if you will read these notes, but I'll keep leaving them for you. I hope someday you'll understand my words and the madness will fade from your mind.

In this strange and dark place, we can find light and purpose. We are not left to just wander alone, craving beauty, power, and other meaningless things. Even the heart of someone feeling incomplete can discover joy. We're not lost. We're merely waiting to be found.

We are so much alike. Formed from the same mold. We're like sisters, you and me. I wish you comfort and the wisdom to let your heart melt into happiness. I won't give up trying to reach you before it's too late.

—a Friend

New Objective:
FIX THE MUSIC BOX

Directly behind you, next to the entrance, you'll see a ladder. Just at the top you'll reach a boarded-up alcove, inside of which is the "He will Return—Sammy Lawrence" memo. There is a Keeper stalking the outside corridor. Stay out of harm's way by dashing over a rickety walkway, collapsing its fragile panels as you go. Balance along the stronger rails to return.

Carefully follow the Keeper around, continuing straight as it turns left at the potted plant. At the end of the corridor is a room with a cabinet that contains the winder for the music box. You may time this just right to be behind the Keeper once more. In any case, go back to the broken walkway and dash across. The Keeper cannot follow you if you're spotted.

You'll see another Keeper on the floor below, however. Wait a short while before following in its tracks to an area with a Gent locked door. There are now two Keepers on the lookout, making it difficult to explore the room that lies beyond. You're looking for the figurine for the music box among the many filing shelves that also shield you from view. Make your way extremely carefully to the section at the back where a small dressing table has a copy of *The Illusion of Living*. The nearby scruffy and secluded study area has the missing figurine. Recharge your Gent pipe at the Gent Charging Station around the corner before you leave.

On your way back to the music box, use the Gent pipe to power down the Security Towers in the panel immediately outside the filing room. You now have those cool powers back. Using Flow, you can reach an area of the upper corridors, across from where you'll find a broken section of railing. You'll see a linker pipe and a bookshelf. Nestled in the corner is a chair, on top of which is the "In Plain Sight—Wilson" audio log. Now fix that music box.

New Objective:
FIND A SPOT TO PLACE THE MUSIC BOX

The music box goes on top of the dressing table, just inside the area where you followed the Keeper in search of the figurine. There is a silhouette to let you know where to set it down. Once activated, the Keepers are drawn to the music box, allowing you to slip by unnoticed. You'll see a South Wing door behind where they stand enthralled. Flip a wall switch and exit. The passageway leads a short way back to Betty, in Wilson's Retreat.

Voice of
WILSON

It's been years and my face is still a mystery to my coworkers. They don't know me. They avoid me as if I carried some infectious disease. At first, this was an insult. But now . . . it is a gift. With the right costume, I can play the part of anyone. I can go completely unnoticed, hidden among the shadowed walls. As a clerk, an artist, a producer. Or even . . . a lowly janitor.

New Objective:

HEAD TO THE FARMER'S MARKET

Betty politely asks that you collect a few ingredients from the Farmer's Market downtown. To get there you'll need to catch the train, which also makes backtracking quite a bit easier. To make this round trip more efficient, there are a few things to do before your departure.

Wilson's Laboratory is now open, at the far end of the corridor behind Betty. On your way down the many flights of stairs, you'll pass a paint spill. Tucked behind the steel drum is one of Drew's *The Illusion of Living* books. Upon reaching Wilson's Laboratory, don't go inside. Instead, take seriously his warning about "where we're going there will be no return . . ." Turn around and plunder the right-hand locker for its copy of *The Illusion of Living*.

INKJETS ROCK!

To attend the Inkjets concert, staged in Artist's Rest, search the dining table where Alice Angel serves her electrifying banquet for one half of a ticket. The second half you'll grab from the Gent Building, above Dishy Cantina—the area where you found "Keeper Log 26." With both in hand, return to Artist's Rest and enjoy the show!

Now catch the train. Upon arrival in the city, there is a locker on the platform to your right. Inside you'll find the "Fashionable Hat" memory. On the bench to the left, against the wall, is the final copy of *The Illusion of Living*. Break the padlocked gate to reach the street exit.

Betty's ingredients are at the Ye Olde Farmer's Market, next to Grand Chops: Choice Meatly Products. The box of "Live Contents" is conveniently waiting on a stool for your collection. Return to Betty, who thanks you for the help and in return points you toward the fountain at the bottom of the stairs where you'll find the "Cracked Mug" memory. Betty also reminds you that Wilson wants to see you. You know that already, you're just taking your time . . .

THE INSANE READER ACHIEVEMENT

When you have all twenty-four copies of *The Illusion of Living*, sit in the chair next to the rainbow light on the way down to Wilson's Laboratory. This will also unlock an alternate ending.

FAMILIAR FACES ACHIEVEMENT

After you've unlocked train travel in Chapter 5, there are ten theMeatly cutouts to find. Each one of them is hidden behind a tatty poster of Boris. You can expect to fight a seemingly endless succession of Lost Ones while searching.

1. Return to the Alice Angel assassination location, and the first stack of boxes Alice gunned down, left of the balcony from where you both fell. In the corridor, above a sofa, is a poster.

2. Follow the passageway beneath the balcony, which snakes left and right. To the right of the "Wilson Knows" poster is a chair and another poster.

3. In the Gent Building, the first room you reach is through the vent (after being gassed by the Keeper in Chapter 4). The "Boris" poster is just behind the table with the covered body.

4. In the alley behind Grand Chops: Choice Meatly Products, high on the brick wall—on your left-hand side as you exit the shop—is a poster that you can only reach using Flow.

5. Next stop is the subway station. Take the emergency shaft back into the sewers then backtrack all the way to the sewer entrance. The poster is on your left as you exit.

6. Flow up the shaft from the Widow King's lair and go to Artist's Rest. Unlock Lost & Found from inside the kiosk. The poster is in the room marked "Flow" at the end of the corridor.

7. Backtrack from Artist's Rest all the way to Animation Alley and the Employee lockers. Take the "Guys" route and look for the poster on your right-hand side at the very back.

8. From Animation Alley, head back through the Screening Room to the drainage pipe where you freed Porter, the Lost One. Just near here is the poster you'll need to step through.

9. Go back to Animation Alley, and the ticket booth area in the Artist Atrium Halls. Enter the office through the hole in the wall next to the Bendy standee. A poster is on the wall inside.

10. Return to the Heavenly Toys Lobby, and the walkway leading to the stairway at the back. Climb up the wall or Flow to the ledge where a wooden chair sits in front of the "Boris" poster.

Shipahoy Dudley

Directions:

When you're ready—after collecting all there is to collect, seeing all there is to be seen, knowing all that can be known—return to Wilson in his laboratory. He outlines plans to dethrone the Ink Demon. The plans mostly involve, ahem, Shipahoy Dudley. After declining the part of Wilson's deal that lets you "live again as a god," you're free to explore once more.

Behind you, in the laboratory entrance, is a locker that has the "Hot dog" memory inside. Next, approach the "Subject Accepted" sign toward the back of the laboratory, and turn right to find a cabinet with "The Bigger Things—Nathan Arch" audio log on its large, lower shelf.

Voice of
NATHAN ARCH

I decided to go for a walk this morning. Took a little stroll down to the park. Enjoyed the warm sun for a while, found a quiet bench, even grabbed a hot dog. It's been ages since I've done that. Tessa would kill me if she knew I've been off my diet. When I got back to the office, I stopped by the animation department and said hello to the troops. My gosh, they're getting younger every day. Either that or I'm just getting older. It all made me realize time is moving on. The hard struggles don't seem as dire as they used to. Life has other value. I think I'll go home early today. Maybe I'll even pick up a hot dog for Tessa.

New Objective:

SHIPAHOY WILSON BOSS BATTLE

Enter the laboratory through the hatch next to the "Subject Accepted" sign. Once inside, throw the lever to summon Shipahoy Wilson, the cursed combination of Shipahoy Dudley and Wilson Arch.

Wilson is armed with a mighty anchor that he swings toward you wherever you stand. This is the key to solving the first part of the puzzle involving four power generators. As Wilson's anchor strikes your starting position beside the rear generator, it smashes the control panel. Use the Gent pipe to deactivate the generator and recharge at the wiring on the facing wall.

Trick Wilson into hurling his anchor at you while standing in front of the intact generators, shutting them down with the Gent pipe when their switches are exposed. After the second is closed, Wilson throws debris, and Lost Ones enter the fray. The wiring current dies until they're all splattered. Wilson gets fired by the Security Towers when the last generator dies.

Your Flow powers have returned, and are needed to evade Wilson's attempts at crushing you with his huge hand or anchor. Each time he misses, rush to whack his back with the Gent pipe. When he flails with the anchor, this exposes his torso and stomach-churning head inside.

Learn the pattern, stay calm, use Flow for a speed advantage when you have it available. This battle doesn't exactly end well for you in the strictest terms—more a noble sacrifice. "It's time, Audrey . . ."

New Objective:

A MONSTER LIKE ME

You and the Ink Demon become one, but you hold the power to break the Cycle: a film reel, marked "The End." Every Lost One and Seeker is out to stop your rampage through the Gent facility, but you sense that this is the home stretch. Find a projector, your final objective.

Smashing through walls, pummeling all before you, it feels easy to begin with. But the Ink Demon taunts you as odds stack against you. Hope starts to fade. At one crucial moment, trapped behind a giant security door, Alice intervenes with her Tommy gun. Her pet "wolf" Tom takes charge of a Lurker, and together you power through more waves of enemies.

At last, you reach what seems to be a dead end. However, Subject 414 joins the effort and tells you that a projector lies just up ahead. Is this really the end, or is it a new beginning . . .?

THE ARCHIVES

Welcome to the Archives! In this extra area you can explore the bewildering band of Bendy's friends and enemies and learn a little bit more about them. Take a look around—you never know who you might bump into . . .